CLASS TRIPPED

MIDDLE SCHOOL MAYHEM BOOK ELEVEN

C.T. WALSH

COVER CREDITS

Cover design by Books Covered
Cover photographs © Shutterstock
Cover illustrations by Maeve Norton

For my Family

Thank you for all of your support

1

My middle school graduation was rapidly approaching. I was only six weeks away from walking out of that monstrosity known as Cherry Avenue Middle School forever. And the rest of the year was gonna be a cakewalk. We only had three weeks left of classes, a few finals, and then spirit week. And within all of that, we would have our eighth-grade class trip. Each year, they got more and more extravagant. I couldn't wait to find out where my class was going. Or more important, where I was going with my girlfriend, Sophie.

I sat in my advisory classroom next to one of my best friends, Just Charles. Yes, that's his name. Not everybody likes to be called Charlie or Chuck. What can I say? He's a sophisticated guy. He and I chatted while we waited for the Pledge and the Speaker of Doom to give us the morning announcements.

I looked over at Just Charles and said, "They're supposed to be announcing the class trip this morning. Where do you think we're going?"

"I ran some calculations last night based on previous

trips and added some behavioral science into the algorithm-"

"Like what?" I interjected. Just Charles was a beast when it came to numbers and computers.

"Basically, just parents wanting to one up each other. That seems to be the motivating factor behind each trip getting more and more extravagant."

"Interesting. What are you projecting?"

"50% chance of Crescent Cove, a 30% chance of Six Flags, and a 20% chance we dine with the Queen of England."

"Hmmm. No disrespect to the Queen, but I'm hoping for Crescent Cove. It seems more fun, plus I'm sure Randy would be super pompous. Maybe even claim to be in line for the throne."

"Crescent Cove would be awesome. I heard they have a chocolate river."

I laughed. "It's not Charlie and the Chocolate Factory."

"But that would be awesome, wouldn't it?"

"Totally."

Jay Parnell chimed in from a seat behind me. "I heard Mrs. Lynch in the main office saying something about water. It's gotta be Crescent Cove."

"Maybe she was just thirsty," I said, not wanting to get my hopes up.

Jay scoffed, seemingly offended that I didn't believe his intel. "She was talking about the trip."

"The Queen does drink a lot of tea," Just Charles said, attempting to defend his wild claim about dining with her.

Jay said, "It's Crescent Cove. I know it."

I took a deep breath and smiled. "I hope you're right. Sophie and I are just gonna relax by the pool. Go for long walks on the beach. Get a couples' massage."

Just Charles chuckled. "They don't do those on a school trip."

"That's okay. Maybe we'll check out some of the waterfalls."

Just Charles smirked. "Maybe hit one of those secluded caves for a little smoochie smoochie?" He proceeded to embarrass himself by making a whole bunch of loud kissing noises. Like I said, he's a really sophisticated guy.

"Knock it off," I said.

And then the Speaker of Doom crackled to life. Our principal, Ms. Armpit Hair, or more properly, Ms. Anne Pierre, spoke. Her voice echoed throughout the room as she said, "I am very excited to announce this year's eighth-grade class trip. You wanted a water adventure, so..."

"Yes, dudes. Yes!" I said, knowing we were going to Crescent Cove, the land of chocolate rivers and cave smooching.

Ms. Armpit Hair continued, "We're going to Rocky River!"

"Yes!" I yelled, jumping out of my seat with my fists in the air.

The whole class groaned and looked at me sideways.

"What did she say?" I asked, confused and deflated. "Did she say Rocky River?"

"Yep," Just Charles said, shaking his head.

I slumped back into my seat. I tried to focus on the positives. "There's not a lot to do, but at least the resort there is decent."

Ms. Armpit Hair added more good news. "But we're not going to go all high class. No, we're going camping!"

Nearly all the girls in the room shrieked, "What?"

I wasn't overly keen on camping, either. I'd probably light myself on fire or get eaten by a bear.

The Speaker of Doom announced more lovely details,

"...No cellphones. No running water. No toilets! It's going to be an amazing trip!"

I looked over at our Advisory teacher, Mrs. Callahan. Even she couldn't fathom what had just happened.

Just Charles looked at me, dumbfounded. He said, "I had Rocky River at a zero percent chance. How is that possible?"

I ran my fingers through my hair, my giant brain still not able to reconcile what just happened. "We're going to *Rotten* River? How could this be?" I asked.

"That place stinks," Jay said.

"Literally," Just Charles said.

"I heard that all the fish have like three eyes and one fin, so they all swim around in circles because of all the pollution," Jay added.

"I'll calculate our survival odds after school today," Just Charles said, making note of it.

Welcome to Cherry Avenue Middle School, where students have to calculate the survival odds of school-sponsored trips. Buckle up. It's gonna be a rocky/rotten ride. Lives could be lost. And I didn't need Just Charles' algorithm to tell me that I would be at the top of the list of potentials.

2

I was so confused and angered by the Rotten River decision that I hadn't paid any attention to the rest of the morning announcements. It wasn't until later that day in health and home economics class that I found out more great news.

We had a few minutes at the end of class to chat before the bell rang. I had a large group of friends in that class. Pretty much all of them, including Sophie and my best friend, Ben Gordon.

Sophie looked at me and said, "What's wrong? You seem out of sorts."

"I'm planning my funeral. Early odds suggest I have only a 40% chance of surviving the class trip."

"That high?" Luke asked, unhelpfully.

"I'm disappointed about the class trip. I was hoping we would go to Crescent Cove together," I said.

Sophie smiled. "Don't worry. It'll be fine."

It wouldn't be fine. At all. But at least she made me feel better at that moment. That is, until Randy Warblemacher, my middle school nemesis, butted into the conversation.

"Hey, Davenfart. Your brother tell you the big baseball news?" Randy said for the entire class to hear.

"The whole Bear Creek pitching staff is taking bets on how many times they can bean you in the head?" I asked.

"What? They are?" Randy asked, shrilly.

"Oh, that wasn't it? Sorry. Don't worry. I'm sure it'll be fine," I said. "Your parents have insurance, though, right? Just in case."

Randy shook off his nervousness, seemingly remembering his purpose for bringing up the subject of baseball in the first place. "Whatever. I'm not afraid of those sissies. They don't even have a Starbucks."

I wasn't sure how not having a Starbucks meant they couldn't throw baseballs at his head, but I didn't care to engage him.

Randy continued, smirking. "You didn't hear the announcement?"

"Nope."

"Well, then you probably don't know that I'm the captain of the baseball team. I beat your brother out. By a long shot."

"I'm ecstatic for you," I said, turning my back to him.

He didn't get the hint. He kept talking as the bell rang and we all headed for the door. "You seem to fancy yourself the leader of the nerds, but I'm a true leader. I've earned it. You can't just name yourself king of the nerds and expect people to follow you." Randy looked at Nick DeRozan and a few other members of his goon squad, snapped his fingers, and said, "Let's go."

The idiots followed Randy down the hall.

I nodded to Ben and Luke and said, loud enough for Randy to hear, "Follow me, boys!"

"Nah, man. I gotta go that way," Luke said.

"Yeah, me, too," Ben said.

They both walked off in the opposite direction.

I looked at Sophie and said, "Could've done without that."

THE REST of the day was pretty much an extension of what I've told you already. The more I thought about the class trip, the more wound up I got. By the time I sat down for dinner with my family, I was flat out ready to explode, bursting with conspiracy theories.

My fork clanked down on the plate as I said, "I'm pretty certain Ms. Pierre is stealing from the school."

"What are you talking about?" my mother asked, as the rest of my family stared at me.

Derek was nodding along with me. Finally, we agreed on something.

I didn't answer the question. I just compounded the confusion. "Oh, and she's also trying to kill me."

After my father finished choking, he sternly asked, "Austin, tell me what's going on."

I backtracked a little. "How else can you explain our class trip? The school bank account has been drained. That's why we have to go camping on Rotten River. And if you wanted to take out a student, but make it look like an accident, what better way to do it than to send them out to be eaten by lions, tigers, and bears?"

"There aren't lions and tigers there," my father said.

"But there *are* bears," I countered.

"Bear assassins," Derek said, laughing. I guess he was no longer on my side.

"Nobody is trying to kill you," my father said. "You'll be fine. You might get a little wet and a little dirty, but you will get through it. I'm sure they'll have some great guides. You might even be surprised by how much fun you have."

"I doubt that," I said, beginning to eat again. "I'm gonna look like an idiot in front of Sophie."

Derek laughed. "Umm, that's every day."

"Derek," my mother said.

"Who the heck wants to go rafting and camping for a class trip?" Leighton shook her head and continued, "I would never do that."

"What was your trip?" Derek asked. The dumb kid never pays attention to anything that doesn't involve him.

"We went to NYC and saw Harry Potter on Broadway. It was spectacular."

"How is this fair? I'm definitely gonna get eaten by a bear," I said. I was certain of it. I almost wanted it to happen, just to prove everyone wrong.

"It'll be a disappointed bear with those twiggy legs," Derek said.

"Thanks for your concern."

AGAINST MY BETTER JUDGMENT, I did sign up for the trip. Sophie wanted to go. So, at least she would be there, and the rest of my crew. Plus, we would miss school on Friday, which had to be better than actually being in school. True, I didn't fear for my life on most days in school, except for Wedgie Wednesdays, but at least there would be some excitement in my day. I was tired of the monotony. Might as well get chased by bears to spice things up.

It was the night before my funeral. Just after dinner, I remembered that I should probably have some equipment, or at least a few changes of clothes. Particularly underwear. No reason. I slid into the den while my mother was folding laundry.

"Mom, did you pack my bag for the trip?" I asked. "I can't find it anywhere," I said, annoyed.

"No," she said, simply.

"Why not?"

"Because you're not a baby."

"That's questionable," Leighton said from the kitchen.

"What about lunch for the bus?"

"Make yourself a sandwich," she said, not even looking up at her baby boy.

Derek stomped through the kitchen and shouldered me out of the way. "Mom! I thought you said you were gonna put my laundry on my bed?"

"I haven't gotten to that yet. I'm not done folding it yet. *For you.*"

"Unbelievable," Derek muttered.

My mother huffed and threw down a pair of Derek's folded underwear, which promptly unfolded. I don't know why people fold underwear. It seems pointless, but whatever. My mother looked at both of us. "You know, you two could be a little more appreciative about the things your father and I do for you."

"What's that?" Derek asked.

My mother threw down another piece of folded laundry. "You know, I can't wait until the baby is born. At least she won't complain that I don't do enough for her."

I furrowed my brow. "Won't she cry every time she wants something from you?"

"Yes, but that's what babies do."

Derek was his typical smart self. "Austin still cries all the time."

"Do not," I said, really maturely.

"Now, we'll have two babies," Derek said, laughing.

"Well, your brother is gonna have to grow up. And you, too."

Derek ignored the last part, looked at me with a smirk, and asked, "You potty trained yet? You *were* still wearing diapers in sixth grade." He was referring to the time I wore a diaper to stake out Sophie's house to win her back. It was a success, so I make no apologies.

"Ha. Ha," I fake laughed. "Very funny," I said, disappearing into the kitchen.

I caught myself before asking my mother to make me a sandwich. I nearly tore open the fridge, grabbed the cheese and bread, and tossed it onto the counter. I made one of my favorite culinary delights. You guessed it. A cheese sandwich. But there was no joy in making this sandwich. I nearly smushed the normally-spongy potato bread flatter than a sheet of paper. I slammed the cheese onto that bread like I was trying to melt it into the bread by sheer velocity. I grabbed a plate and plopped down into a chair at the kitchen table, sulking while eating my smushed cheese sandwich.

I chomped on my cheese and bread, stewing about my conversation with my mother, angry that she couldn't even make me a sandwich on the eve of my eternal demise. They even give murderers on Death Row a last meal of their choice. When love isn't an ingredient in the recipe, it's just cheese and bread. When you add love, you make a meal. At least that's what my Gammy always says. But what does she know? She orders takeout all the time. I think I was losing it or my mind had never been more clear. I wasn't sure.

I took a few bites and reached for my glass of water. It wasn't there. "Dang it," I said, annoyed.

"What's the matter?" my mother asked, walking into the room.

"I forgot to pour myself some water. Can you grab me one?"

"I'm pregnant. You get *me* a drink," she said, even more annoyed than my own annoyance.

"You know, I may be about to die on this trip and you don't even care. I guess you'll be fine. I mean, we've got a new baby on the way. You'll probably forget my name by Christmas."

"Austin, knock it off," my mother said. Before she could say anything else, the doorbell rang. "Ooh, that must be the decorator. She's here for the baby's room." She left in the middle of our conversation, heading off to more important things than me. Things like fluffy pillows, paint colors, and curtains.

I shook my head, as I watched her leave. I muttered to myself and then gobbled up another bite.

My father walked in and did a double take. "What's the matter? You look depressed."

"I'm about to meet my doom. And even if I survive this weekend, I'm going to be replaced."

"You're not going to die on a school camping trip. And what is this talk about being replaced?"

"Emily is coming. We all know Mommy wanted me to be a girl. That's why she used to dress me up as Little Bo Peep after Leighton grew up."

"Yeah, that was a little weird, but nobody is replacing you, bud," my father said, sliding into the chair next to me. He looked at my mangled food and said, "Wow. You're eating a cheese sandwich and you're mad? I don't know what to make of this."

I wasn't going to get into the whole sandwich, meals, and love conundrum. I didn't have the patience. "Even if I'm not *replaced*, I'm going to be the least-liked kid in the family."

"What are you talking about?" my dad said with a chuckle.

I wasn't enthused by how cavalier he was being about my family standing. "Leighton is your first born and has the family butt chin. Derek has a lot of room for improvement, but also has the family butt chin. And if the sonogram is to be believed, Emily will have the biggest butt chin in the entire family *and* will be the baby of the group. Where does that leave me? Third born with no butt chin. I can't think of a worse situation. How is that fair?"

"Life isn't always fair-"

I interrupted, "Don't I know it."

Derek walked into the kitchen from the den, peering over a teetering pile of laundry. "This is unbelievable. I can't believe I have to do this," he muttered.

My father looked at both of us, shook his head, and sternly said, "With the baby coming, it's time for you two to grow up."

Derek had no idea what was going on. "I'm putting on muscle like a freak, Dad. Mr. Muscalini has me eating protein like a caveman." He navigated the island in the kitchen, not stopping to chat.

"I'm not talking about physically growing up. I'm talking about maturing as a human being."

"Why the heck would I want to do that?" I said.

"Because you can't be a forty year old baby," my father said, simply.

"Nobody's told your father that," my mother said, entering the room, and grabbing a stack of clothes from Derek.

"Hey," my father whined.

Derek and my mother disappeared with the laundry, leaving my father and me alone again.

"All I have is that I'm the baby," I said, not looking at him.

"You're a teenager."

"Still, I have to cling on to something. That's the only place I fit in this family. Without that, I just don't know where I fit."

"Of course you fit in."

"No, I don't," I said with a huff. "I have to pack. Mom would rather move the crib around the baby's room fifty times than help me." I stood up and headed for my room.

"Austin-" my father said, his shoulders slumping.

My mother returned to the kitchen just as I was leaving. I growled at her as I passed.

She looked at my father and said, "I've never been so happy that the kids are going away."

"Gee, thanks," I muttered.

3

I stood in the foyer of my house with my brother and father, packed bags at our feet. I was conflicted. I didn't want to go, but didn't want to stay after what my mother had said. I had a full night's sleep, but felt no better about it.

My father looked at Derek and me and said, "Well, it's time to skedaddle."

"I don't know what that means," Derek said.

"Time to go. The wilderness is waiting."

"I'm so pumped," I said, deflated.

My father laughed. "It won't be so bad."

It would be.

"Did you say goodbye to your mother?"

Derek nodded.

"Yep," I lied.

Leighton and my mother walked out of the kitchen into the foyer.

"Have a good trip, boys," my mother said.

"Thanks," Derek said. "See you on Sunday."

I looked into my mother's eyes, my heart racing. "Enjoy

your time without me. I know you've been counting the minutes until I leave. And I'm sure counting the minutes until the baby is born and I'm replaced." I grabbed my backpack and walked out the door without waiting for a response.

"Austin," my mother called after me.

I kept going. Outside, I nearly tore the car door off its hinges. I plopped into my seat, my backpack on my lap.

Derek hopped into the back seat beside me.

My father slipped into the car. He turned to look at me in the back seat. "Are you sure that's how you want to leave things? I don't want you to regret it."

"She's the one who should have the regrets. Let's go. I don't want to miss the bus," I said, rolling my eyes. "If she cared so much, perhaps she would've actually come after me."

"She's pregnant. She's very tired. And you two could help out more. We're not your servants."

"Uh, huh," I said, not caring.

"Okay. Suit yourself," my father said, kicking the car into gear.

We rode to school without saying a word to each other. I stared out the window with my arms crossed. By the time we arrived, the school parking lot was bursting with activity. Kids with oversized backpacks were spinning in circles, knocked off course by other kids spinning in circles. I wondered who was the first kid to start the domino effect. It didn't take long for me to figure it out. I saw Just Charles standing with Cheryl, Luke, and Ben. Just Charles wore a ginormous pack on his back and one strapped to his chest. He wobbled from side to side, knocking into everyone and everything.

I walked over to them, my father at my heels.

Just Charles' eyes lit up when he saw me. He threw his hand up into a wave and promptly fell over, crashing to the ground with a whole lot of clanking and crunching.

Cheryl and Ben attempted to help him up, while I rushed over.

"I'm okay. I'm okay," Just Charles said.

I looked over at the parents congregating. Just Charles' father, Mr. Zaino, was shaking his head, seemingly not sure whether to laugh or cry.

His mother rushed to Just Charles. "My baby!"

Just Charles was back on his feet, stabilized by Cheryl and Ben. Just Charles' mother dusted off his clothes and then fixed his hair.

I shook my head. "That sounded like cookies. That's very disappointing. Probably the only worthwhile thing you brought."

"I have everything we need and more," Just Charles said.

"And more is right," Cheryl said.

Just Charles said, "Mom, can we run to the store real quick and get more cookies?"

"Sure thing, honey."

My father looked at her, disapprovingly. "I don't think there's time. The bus is leaving in a few minutes."

"Aww, man," I said. "What? Those cookies sounded good."

All the parents joined the conversation. Ben's dad, Mr. Gordon, stepped forward. "Be safe out there. Listen to your guides. And maybe try to grow up a little bit."

"I expect you to move out and get your own place by Monday," my father said. "Or at least pay me rent."

"I'm thirteen! I don't want to grow up. I want to be a kid forever," I said.

"Me, too. I'm proud to be a momma's boy," Just Charles said, his mother beaming.

Mr. Gordon shook his head. "You guys are gonna be in a world of hurt."

Mr. Zaino looked at my father. "Have you ever taken your boys camping?"

"No. You?"

"Nope. I feel like a failure as a father," Mr. Zaino said.

"They're not gonna make it. They're too soft," Mr. Gordon whispered.

"We can hear you," Ben said.

Our dads shrugged. Mr. Gordon looked at Ben and said, "Just try not to embarrass yourself. Or me."

"Thanks for the great pep talk, Dad."

"Let's not be too hard on these boys," Mrs. Zaino said. She licked her finger and then proceeded to rub something off Just Charles' face.

Mr. Zaino closed his eyes, as if praying for strength.

Mrs. Zaino handed Just Charles twenty dollars. "Here. Buy some cookies when you get there."

Before Mr. Zaino could say anything, the familiar voice of one Mr. Muscalini, our esteemed gym teacher, said, "Money ain't gonna buy nothin' in the wilderness, y'all. I reckon Charles here is gonna be a man by the time he returns to ya, ma'am."

"Why is he talking like that?" Cheryl asked me.

I shrugged. I never could figure out the complex man that is Mr. Muscalini.

Mrs. Zaino's eyes widened and her voice rose an octave. "What are you going to do to him?"

Mr. Muscalini put his hands on his hips and said, "I ain't gonna do nothin' to him, ma'am. The wild is either gonna break 'im or make 'im."

"You protect my baby," Mrs. Zaino said, a little too loud for Just Charles' liking.

"We'll be fine, Mommy. Er, Mom," Just Charles said, puffing out his chest, and nearly falling backward, before Ben caught him.

The dads all just shook their heads, disappointed. Their confidence in us was inspiring.

"Where are the rest of the girls?" I asked Cheryl.

Luke looked up from his phone. "I'm texting Dayna now."

"I'll text Sammie," Ben said.

I felt left out, so I grabbed my phone and texted Sophie. I looked up when I heard a bunch of parents huff. Mr. Muscalini nearly blew me down with his lungs. For all his muscles, he must hit the cardio pretty hard, too.

"Y'all gonna leave them cellphones. You won't need 'em."

"What?" Luke shrieked. He held his cellphone to his chest and wrapped his arms around it like it was a baby. "I can't do that."

"You'll survive," my father said, laughing.

"Everybody is gonna survive without their cellphones," Mr. Gordon added.

Mr. Muscalini chimed in with his newfound accent, "Mmm, I reckon not all these youngsters are gonna make it." He used his head to point to Ben and me.

"I'm sure the teachers and guides have phones. It'll be good for you to disconnect," Mr. Gordon said.

"Hand them over," my father said, his hand out for mine. "Kiss them goodbye if you must."

Ben kissed his phone and handed it to his father.

Randy called over from another group, "Hey, Gordo! That's the most action you've gotten in your life. Unless kissing your mother counts."

I looked at my father and said, "See what we deal with every day?"

"That's middle school for ya," my dad said. Mr. Muscalini's accent must've been rubbing off on him. I hoped we wouldn't come back on Sunday all talking like a bunch of cowboys.

"Let's go. Hand 'em over," Mr. Zaino said.

Luke's thumbs were going crazy on his phone. "Let me just play one more minute. I'm about to pass level 2027!"

Mr. Muscalini returned to himself and said, "At some point, I'm just gonna have to admit that I failed to turn these boys into men. It's never happened before. But, look at them. I mean, can you blame me?" he asked my father. "Not once have they ever had a protein shake. Not once! So, I blame them."

"What's protein?" Ben asked, egging Mr. Muscalini on.

Mr. Muscalini face palmed himself, and like an old lady said, "Oy!" He turned his back and walked away.

We all handed in our phones. Just Charles leaned over to me. "Don't worry, I bought a burner phone. It's in my pack."

"I hope it didn't get crunched."

I heard shushing behind me, so I turned around. Ms. Armpit Hair stood at the bottom of a bus step, peering out at the rest of us in the parking lot. It was funny to see her dressed down in a sweatsuit and a ponytail. Normally, she was impeccably dressed, and none of it ever impeded her ability to do anything. I'd once seen her do a front flip and land with high heels at our custodian Zorch's wedding. "May I have your attention? Thank you, everyone, for coming. We are about to embark on the adventure of a lifetime. It's a mission, really. A mission to prepare these fine young minds for the challenges that lie ahead in high school."

"By drowning us in a polluted river?" Luke asked.

A few people chuckled. A lot of people nodded in agreement.

"Nonsense, children. That was a long time ago. The river is perfectly acceptable, as far as you know." Ms. Armpit Hair continued, "We decided to forego the extravagant trips of the past because in today's day and age, we think children should play more outside, connect with nature, and learn to socialize face to face. That means no cellphones."

The crowd groaned.

Mr. Gifford, Cherry Avenue's science teacher, scratched his head and said, "I thought it was a budget issue?"

"Not at all true. Now, say goodbye to your parents and turn your phones over to them. We'll be checking students for phones and other contraband."

Without warning, Mr. Muscalini wailed on his whistle, nearly blasting my eardrums to smithereens and perhaps even waking the dead at the local cemetery. We had been conditioned to run with reckless abandon at the sound of a whistle, so kids were trampling each other to get to the bus line.

Mr. Muscalini's voice boomed, "Let's go, Gordo! Mommy's not gonna be able to wipe your butt on this trip!"

Ben's pack bounced on his back as he ran. "Sir, my mother never wipes my butt!"

"That's questionable, son. Now get on the bus."

Our pack merged in with Sophie, Sammie, and Ditzy Dayna as we headed to the bus. Ben looked at Sammie and said, "I swear. She does *not* wipe my butt." Sammie wasn't convinced, so Ben continued, dragging me into the mess, "He's the one who wore the diaper in sixth grade!"

"It was once!" I yelled. I looked at Sophie, "And it was for love."

The girls just shook their heads as we slowed down and fell into the line. Teachers and security guards were searching backpacks and other bags for cellphones and other contraband.

Thankfully, Mr. Muscalini was our bus monitor instead of one of the security guards. As tough as Mr. Muscalini was, he wasn't nearly as tough as security. And I'd had my share of run ins with security. I wanted no part of them, even though I wasn't even trying to smuggle anything on the trip. Honest.

I heard Randy talking behind me. I stared forward and kept my head down, as we shuffled forward. Eventually, we got to Mr. Muscalini. He did a cursory search of my bag and tossed it under the bus.

Mr. Muscalini looked at all of us and said, "It's game time, boys. The objective is to win."

"Win what?" Ben asked.

"Win at life," he said, simply.

We all looked at each other, confused. I *was* going to try not to die, but I wasn't sure that's what he meant.

For once, Mr. Muscalini picked up that we had no idea what he was talking about, so he added some clarification. "It's time to grow up, gentlemen. Use this as an opportunity to grow as men. To put it in nerd terms that you'd understand, just think of it like you, 2.0."

"We don't really want to grow up," I said, shrugging.

Mr. Muscalini's shoulders slumped.

Randy's voice interjected behind us, "Figures. I, for one, can't wait to grow up and leave all you punks behind. But you can come watch me play when I'm in the NBA or the NFL. I haven't decided which one."

Randy's tough guy routine fizzled quickly, though. As his mother passed by our line, she called out to him, "Mommy loves you, Randy Pandy Bear! Be safe."

I turned around and smiled at Randy. He smirked at his mother and then rolled his eyes at Regan next to him.

"What are you looking at, Davenfart?"

"You didn't say goodbye to your mommy, Randy Pandy," I said to laughs. I got on the bus before he could respond.

Sophie followed me onto the bus and then the rest of the crew one by one. Just Charles entered the bus like a huge weight had been lifted off his shoulders, which it had. He gave me a thumbs up, as he slipped into the seat across from mine.

Just Charles whispered, "Burner phone remains in my custody."

"Nice," I said.

Ditzy Dayna walked onto the bus with Luke. She looked around like she had just completed the heist of the century. "Can you believe that they let me bring my hairdryer?"

"That's great news," Luke said, enthusiastically. Once Dayna sat down and was out of sight, he shrugged with a smile.

I had the pleasure of sitting with Sophie on the bus. And the displeasure of sitting behind Mr. Gifford and Mrs. Funderbunk. Although, I did find it humorous from time to time. Mr. Gifford had a serious crush on Mrs. Funderbunk, but she didn't share his enthusiasm for their coupleage. Perhaps you remember the Valentine's Day rejection that caused him to carry around his tuna salad in his overgrown beard for a few days.

Mr. Gifford leaned over to Mrs. Funderbunk, who looked less than enthused to be there and with him, and said, "There's something primal about camping out, where men and women can forget about bank accounts and social standing and just connect like the ancients did."

Mrs. Funderbunk said, "No, there's not."

"You're right, Madeline, but there's something romantic about being in the great outdoors, don't you think?"

"You mean with the bugs and pooping in holes?" Mrs. Funderbunk said, nearly regurgitating breakfast.

"Pooping in holes," Mr. Gifford repeated, laughing. "Wait, what? We're pooping in holes?"

The rest of the ride pretty much went like that.

4

We arrived at Rocky River. We would separate into groups, a few students and a teacher, and raft a few miles down the river before making camp for the night. When we got off the buses, a tour company was packing up the rafts with gear from students that had arrived on earlier buses. We waited in line to be outfitted with the most glamorous of orange life vests before being plopped into a bag of air and sent down a polluted river. Fear and disgust emanated from our pores, which was probably the emotions Ms. Armpit Hair was going for when she planned our trip.

And that was before Randy started running his mouth. Again. "Listen up, everybody. I've got ten bucks that says Davenfart gets eaten by a bear."

"I'm not taking that bet," somebody said from the crowd. "Davenport is totally getting eaten by a bear."

"I'll take that bet," Derek said.

"Really, dude?" I asked.

"What?" Derek scoffed. "I'm betting you won't get eaten."

"I do appreciate that, but why are you playing into his stupid games?" I asked.

"Because I want to crush Randy and take his ten bucks. That's why I do most things," Derek said.

"Anybody else?" Randy said.

A bunch of kids surrounded Randy, haggling and making deals.

"What an idiot," Sophie said.

"Whatever," I said, annoyed, but pretending not to be.

We stepped forward. Some goofy high school kid slapped a beautiful orange life vest over my head, nearly ripping off an ear. I guess they weren't into a great customer experience. You'll realize that as my story continues.

A huge, rugged outdoorsman walked toward us. We all took a step back. He was dressed like a jungle guide with a huge brimmed hat and looked like he could kill us all with just a hard glare.

"This guy is the Mr. Muscalini of the outdoors," Ben said.

"Who's this Mr. Muscalini you speak of?" the guide asked.

"He's our gym teacher. He's over there," I said, pointing in Mr. Muscalini's direction.

"It's more likely that he's the Colt Reddington of the gymnasium," the man boomed while puffing out his chest.

"Who's Colt Reddington?" Sophie asked.

"Why me, of course! Your guide to the adventure of a lifetime!" Colt smiled. I swear his tooth dinged like in TV commercials. "You haven't heard of me?"

"Oh, yeah. Absolutely," Luke said.

"Wonderful," Colt said.

Colt adjusted the life vest around my neck. "This one is a little big. It'll help you float better."

"Not if I slip out of it," I said.

"Fingers crossed that doesn't happen. We've lost kids to the river monster before. Sometimes, we take bets on who that's gonna be."

"Oh, great!" I said.

Mr. Muscalini walked over to us. "One of these days you'll listen to me and you'll eat some protein. You can start right now. There's a bug right there." He pointed down to some sort of beetle running across the dirt. "Crunchy protein is yummy protein." Mr. Muscalini grabbed the beetle and shoved it into my face. "Eat up, Davenport."

"No, thanks, sir. I just ate."

Mr. Muscalini tossed the beetle in his mouth and crunched it with a smile. The smile quickly disappeared. He bent over at the waist and spit out the mangled beetle and wiped his mouth with his sleeve.

Colt looked at Mr. Muscalini with pity. "Amateur. This fool is going to lead a group of children? I feel bad for whoever that is."

I looked at the rest of my group. "Yeah, I think that's us."

Colt stepped toward the river and a larger group of kids. "Greetings, riverfolk!" he said, cheerily. "A few ground rules before we send you off down the river. Don't swim in the water. Don't smell the water. You should probably hold your breath."

"For sixteen miles?" I asked.

Sammie looked at the water and nearly puked. "Who would swim in this water?"

Colt continued, "And whatever you do, don't drink the water."

Before we could question why the heck we were there, Colt looked at Mrs. Funderbunk and said, "And this one looks like she could walk on water."

"Oh, you flatter Mrs. Funderbunk. And she likes it. Please continue," Mrs. Funderbunk said, batting her eyelashes.

Mr. Gifford walked past the tour guide and whispered, "Back off, Bucko. She's mine."

"You think a woman like that could ever go for a man like you?" Colt questioned with a laugh.

Before Mr. Gifford could answer, Mr. Muscalini interrupted. "You trying to tell him about the benefits of protein stacks and super sets? You're wasting your time." Mr. Muscalini looked at Colt's oversized arm and squeezed it. "Impressive." Mr. Muscalini rolled up his sleeves to his shoulders. "Sun's out, guns out. Am I right, bro?"

"Not with this heat, you're not. You better protect that skin or you'll be sorry."

Mr. Muscalini looked like his mother just died.

"Everybody ready?" Colt asked.

There were a whole bunch of less-than-enthusiastic responses.

We followed Colt to the edge of the river. The rafts were being loaded with equipment and kids, and then shipped out.

Just Charles was barely able to maintain his balance. He stood in an abnormally-wide stance, like he was doing yoga. I guess whatever works.

Unfortunately, Mrs. Funderbunk would be the adult in my raft. She wasn't my favorite teacher by a long shot. She was self-centered, played favorites (mainly my nemesis, Randy), and had poor taste in those favorites. Sophie, Just Charles, and Cheryl would be joining us.

I looked behind us to see Mr. Gifford with Randy, Regan, Derek, Jayden, and Nick. I felt bad for Mr. Gifford, having to travel with that crew. It also meant they were all going to be sticking close to us on account of Mrs. Funderbunk, if he could maintain control.

Mr. Muscalini slapped Ben on his shoulder. "You're coming with me, Gordo. It's about time you become a man."

Ben looked like he might break down. "But sir, I already had my bar mitzvah."

"Bless you," Mr. Muscalini said. He wrapped his arm around Ben's shoulder, looking down the river with a smile.

Ben looked at me, confused. I just shrugged. Better him than me.

"Take a big whiff of the great outdoors, Gordo!"

"I don't think that's a great idea-"

"Do it, Gordo!"

Ben took a deep breath and then nearly hacked up half his lung. Mr. Muscalini didn't even notice, as he continued admiring the less-than-beautiful surroundings.

"There you go. Take in this beautiful mountain air. It's so peaceful. Spiritual, even."

"It may bring me closer to God, but death by asthma is not what I'm looking for on this trip, sir."

Colt steadied an oversized round raft at the edge of the river for us. I stepped over the side and into the raft. Just Charles handed me his backpack. I thought I was going to plunge right through the bottom of the raft into the Rotten River. It caught me by such surprise that I dropped the backpack on my foot.

"Owww!" I yelled.

"You've really done a great job with this crew," Colt whispered to Mr. Muscalini.

"There's not much that can be done when they want to stay nerds."

Colt shrugged in agreement.

"Charles, what the heck is in here?" I asked, annoyed.

"Everything he's every owned, apparently," Sophie said, chuckling. "Is your foot okay?"

"I'll live," I said.

"That's debatable," Mr. Muscalini said. "It's a bear-eat-boy world out there."

"Why does everyone think I'm gonna get eaten by a bear?" I asked, angrily.

The goofy kid who nearly ripped my ear off like a savage handed Colt two tents.

Colt looked at me. "Put these under the netting in the center of the raft."

I took the tents and did as I was told. He followed with some water jugs.

"What about food?" Sophie asked.

Colt said, "He's getting some, but we have a supply raft with cooking gear and the main meals."

Mrs. Funderbunk approached the raft and held out her hand to Colt like she was the Queen of England or something.

"Your chariot awaits, my dear. And I await your arrival at the camp site with great anticipation. I'd like to take you on a hike, perhaps explore some caves," Colt said.

Mrs. Funderbunk didn't appear too keen on what had been proposed.

Just Charles leaned over and whispered, "I think he means smoochie smoochie."

"Oh, my," Mrs. Funderbunk said. She didn't respond to just Charles, but based on the batting of her eyelashes and her cheeks' pinkish hue, it was pretty obvious she wanted to join Colt on that 'hike'.

She sat down on the edge of the raft, her cheeks still pink.

Cheryl looked at Colt and said, "I'm nervous. I've never done this before."

"Don't worry about it. Just tuck your feet under the rope, hold on for dear life, and hope none of the rocks slice your raft and you end up like a gutted fish. Have fun!" Colt pushed the raft off into the river, sending four nerds and a drama teacher to a wet, smelly doom. I preferred dry and sweet-smelling doom.

The ride started off okay. We just floated down the middle of the river without having to do much. There were at least a dozen rafts in our general vicinity. We all just kind of bumped each other back into place. We weren't moving very fast, and there was not much of a breeze, so with the sun beating down on us, it was starting to get a little uncomfortable.

I wiped the sweat of my forehead. "It's gonna be a hot one today," I said.

"I'm more concerned about who farted," Just Charles said.

Everybody looked at me, even Mrs. Funderbunk.

"It's the *river*," I said. "It really is rotten."

Everybody continued to stare at me. "I didn't fart. Honest." I was happy to know I could blame all my farts on the river. My favorite author, C.T. Walsh, would be proud. If you recall, when I met him at Comic Con, he blamed everything on barking tree frogs. Yes, he's a weirdo, I know. But also a genius.

Mrs. Funderbunk looked at us and shrugged. "This isn't so bad. I thought it would be worse."

"It's not hard when you're not paddling," Just Charles said, annoyed.

Mrs. Funderbunk scoffed. "Mrs. Funderbunk doesn't do manual labor. Here, Austin. You can have two paddles."

"I can barely paddle one, let alone two."

"Suit yourself. I guess we can put this to use somehow." Mrs. Funderbunk thought for a moment. "Wonderful idea, Mrs. Funderbunk. Let's sing show tunes as we head down the river!"

"Do we have to?" I asked.

Mrs. Funderbunk grabbed the handle of her paddle and used it as a microphone. "Who knows Muddy Water from the musical Big River about Huckleberry Finn?" she asked, excitedly.

"Nobody knows that," Sophie said, politely.

I was in total agreement with Sophie. I was pretty certain whatever Mrs. Funderbunk said wasn't even a thing.

Things continued on for the next twenty minutes with little excitement. We just floated down the river while Mrs. Funderbunk sulked over our show tunes rejection. But then the river started to speed up and things got interesting.

"Whoah, we're definitely gaining speed," Cheryl said.

"How do we control this?" Mrs. Funderbunk said.

Sophie and I looked at each other and jointly said, "We don't."

I took a deep breath and braced for impact, as we headed for a collision with a raft filled with Mr. Gifford and the most hated couple in middle school history, Randy and Regan. Along for the ride with them were Derek, his best friend Jayden, and Nick DeRozan. I tried to stay as far away as possible from all of them. Well, at least when the forces of nature weren't slamming me into them.

Mr. Gifford seemingly had no control, which was not surprising, given that crew.

"Randy, steer left!" he yelled.

Randy ignored him and steered right. "You steer left!

Derek, stop working against us and Jayden, pick up the pace. I carry you guys on the baseball field and in the river!"

"That's why you're the star, Captain Randy baby," Regan said.

I almost vomited, but thankfully, the collision took my attention away from Randy's regurgitational pet name. We were all jolted forward toward the impact zone. A paddle cut through the air like a helicopter blade, heading straight for my beautiful brain. Instinctively, I ducked. Surprisingly, my reflexes actually served me well and were fast enough to avoid the vicious blow. Just Charles' reflexes were not as kind.

After a clank, I heard him say, "Owwww!" He may have also said, "I want my mommy," but it was kind of muffled, so I'm not sure.

Cold water splashed in every direction, soaking all of us. And given the quality of water in Rotten River, perhaps exposing us to toxic chemicals. Fingers crossed I make it through high school without growing an extra arm or a face full of boils.

Mr. Gifford called over to Mrs. Funderbunk, "Fancy meeting you here, Madeline!" I guess he didn't know we were about to die thirty minutes into our school trip.

Before I could get settled from the first collision, we spun around, headed down the river backwards, and bashed into a giant rock. We bounced off with another chilling splash and headed back toward the center of the river.

"We've got to stay away from those rocks!" Sophie yelled. "Colt said they could slice our raft!"

"Steer right!" I yelled. "Why are we going in circles?"

I turned to my right to see Cheryl leaning over the side of the raft with only Just Charles' head and arms in sight.

"Just Charles got bounced from the raft!" I yelled, not sure what to do.

I looked at the only adult in the raft for assistance, but Mrs. Funderbunk was ghost white and looked like she might need a diaper. Or perhaps it was too late for that.

Sophie scooted around the edge of the raft, careful not to take her feet out from under the rope encircling the raft. I followed her, as we spun in circles. Sophie grabbed one of Just Charles' arms while Cheryl had the other. I leaned over the edge of the raft and pulled him by the life vest. We pulled, grunted, and groaned, and I may have let out a squeaker of a fart, although it could've been the Rotten River for all you know, but it was all useless. We couldn't get him back into the raft.

"Let's just hold him until the river slows down!" I yelled.

Then Mrs. Funderbunk ruined my plan. She yelled, "Rocks!"

I looked up over Just Charles to find us rapidly approaching two giant rocks, each standing at least four feet out of the water. I felt the blood drain from my face.

"Am I gonna die?" Just Charles asked in a panic. He didn't wait for an answer. "I want to be buried next to my pet hamster, Orville Hamsterbocker. I bequeath to you, Austin, all my PlayStation games. Cheryl, my love..."

"Shut up and kick!" Cheryl yelled.

"Everybody pull as hard as you can. Now!" Sophie yelled.

We all pulled with every fiber of our beings.

Just Charles let out a scream while we pulled him into the raft. He toppled down on the rest of us. Within a split second, the raft smashed into the rocks. Mrs. Funderbunk shrieked in fear. Had we not already been lying on the bottom of the raft, we would've been jolted off our feet, and perhaps back into Rotten River.

But we were safe. At least for that moment.

"Thanks, guys," Just Charles said, relieved, as we lay on the bottom of the raft, still in a pile.

"I'm so glad you're safe," Cheryl said.

I held my nose and said with a nasal tone, "You're welcome, but next time, shower."

"It's the river!" Just Charles said, defensively.

"Sure it is," Sophie said, laughing.

"I think my clothes are disintegrating."

"This is exhausting," Mrs. Funderbunk said, wiping her brow.

I just shook my head with a chuckle. She just sat there while the rest of us saved Just Charles. But we didn't have any time to complain. We were heading for another impact. I looked up to see Mr. Gifford and the rest of his crew heading straight toward us. We bounced off them and headed down the river next to them.

Randy looked over at me and yelled, "It's a race! Let's go, Davenfart! We're gonna crush you!" He started paddling like mad. "Nick, pick up the pace!"

"It's not a race, idiot," I said, not paddling.

"It is if I say it is." Randy turned to Derek and Jayden and said, "It's a race! Let's go." He looked at me and said, "That's leadership, Davenfart."

Derek looked at me and rolled his eyes.

"More like losership," I said.

As much as I didn't like Randy, I didn't mind Derek having to deal with him and all his annoyingness. Before Randy, my brother was my arch nemesis. We still battle from time to time, but my rivalry with Randy is at a whole new level.

"Let's race them," Sophie said.

"We can't beat them down the river," I said.

"Yeah," Just Charles added. "They have five of the best athletes in the school. And we have, well, us."

"Just let them go," I said.

"That's weak, Davenfart!" Randy said, as they sped away from us.

Mrs. Funderbunk looked at us and said, "That Randy is such a nice boy."

Just Charles muttered, "What world is she living in?"

Mrs. Funderbunk always had a soft spot for Randy, given his golden singing voice. Apparently, she didn't see the dark heart that came along with it. She only saw him as her ticket to the bright lights of Broadway. It was rumored that she was trying to get the high school drama job, so that she could ride Randy's coattails for another four years.

We continued on, the flowing river doing most of the work. We paddled here and there, but it wasn't too difficult.

"This is actually kind of relaxing," I said.

"And the sun isn't so bad anymore," Cheryl said.

"Yeah, my butt crack stopped sweating," Just Charles said, obviously providing a little T.M.I.- too much information from Mr. Sophistication.

"Gross," Cheryl said.

"Nice one, Charles," I said.

Sophie just shook her head, disapprovingly.

"The sun isn't so bad," I agreed. I looked up. "Uh, oh."

"What's wrong?" Mrs. Funderbunk asked.

I didn't answer her right away. My attention was focused on the ginormous storm clouds that seemed to appear out of nowhere and floated right above us.

"The weather doesn't look good," I said. I called out to Mr. Gifford ahead, "Look at that storm cloud."

He looked up and then over at Mr. Muscalini, who was the only one rowing, with Luke, Dayna, Ben, and Sammie just along for the ride. In all fairness, he was so strong, I'm not sure they would help all that much had they actually been trying. Mr. Gifford said, "That doesn't look good!"

"We'll outrun it! Everybody paddle. Double time!"

Mr. Gifford disagreed. "We should take cover until it clears."

"Nonsense! Taking cover is for sissies!" Mr. Muscalini boomed.

"If the river rises, we're not gonna be able to see some of those rocks. We're risking catastrophic failure!"

Mr. Muscalini's voice boomed, as he somehow rowed faster, "I don't believe in failure! We'll just try again."

"That's not what I meant!" Mr. Gifford yelled. "We're gonna sink!"

"I don't believe in sinking!" Mr. Muscalini responded.

"That's not how science works!"

"I know how the science of the mind works!"

Mr. Gifford huffed and turned his focus to his love, Mrs. Madeline Funderbunk. "Madeline, you must hold on as tight as you can. I can't lose you!"

"What? You're a loser?" Mrs. Funderbunk called back.

"I don't think that's what he said," Sophie interjected.

"Do you notice we're starting to go faster?" Cheryl asked.

I looked back behind us. It was pouring and approaching rapidly. "The storm is coming from behind us. It must be filling the river."

The rafts in front of us, which were most of them due to our less-than-athletic team, picked up steam and were seemingly becoming more difficult to control. They were bumping into each other and off of rocks, despite how hard everyone appeared to be rowing.

"We've got to get around that group!" I yelled, pointing to a cluster of rafts that were pinned against some rocks. "Everybody row on the left! Just Charles, use your paddle to steer."

I reached forward with my paddle and thrust it into the water, propelling us forward. I did it again and again, getting into the rhythm. It felt like we were making progress until we hit a big bump and blasted a foot of air. It was just enough of a disruption that my paddle stroke missed the water, so my extremely powerful arms pulled the paddle toward the back of the raft, but met no resistance. I wasn't expecting it, so the momentum of my stroke caused me to lose control of the paddle. It flew behind me and struck Mrs. Funderbunk in the face.

She shrieked and then groaned. I turned around to look at her. She took her hands from her face, blood gushing from her nose. She looked at the blood in her hands and collapsed to the bottom of the raft.

"Oh, my God! Mrs. Funderbunk is dead!" Just Charles yelled in a panic.

5

W e all looked at our bleeding music teacher, not sure what to do.

"She's not dead. She's just unconscious," Sophie said. "But she's still bleeding."

I looked around at the other rafts, trying to figure out where the nearest adult was. Everybody was fighting their own war against nature, but I made eye contact with Mr. Gifford. He must've realized something was wrong.

Mr. Gifford freaked out. "Where's Madeline? My love!"

We steered clear of a bunch of traffic, catching up to the pack.

"Steer toward Mr. Gifford! He'll know what to do!" I yelled.

"That's debatable," Just Charles said, but did as I suggested.

"What happened?" Mr. Gifford asked. "Is she okay?"

"She's fine. Just a bloody nose," I said, downplaying the incident.

"Yeah, Austin broke her nose! Hit her in the face with his paddle!" Just Charles yelled, unhelpfully.

"It was an accident!" I yelled.

Mr. Gifford ignored me. As we approached, he stood up in the raft, attempting to get a better look into the raft. He took a deep breath. I wasn't sure what he was going to do. I'm not sure he even knew. But as we got closer, I heard him whisper, "You got this, Gifford. Be the man you were meant to be. For your lady."

He looked like he needed some help. For what? I didn't know, but I decided to give him some encouragement. "You got this, Mr. Gifford!"

And then I realized he was about to jump into our raft as we moved down the river. He had his foot on top of his raft, ready to launch, but we were drifting apart.

Sophie looked at Mr. Gifford and said, "You don't got this!"

"Don't jump!" I echoed.

He didn't listen. For all the times our teachers yell at us to listen to them, it would've been nice for a little reciprocation.

Mr. Gifford pushed off his front leg on the raft and launched his lanky self into the air, spread eagle, and soaring toward our raft. If we ignore that he left all the students behind that he was supposed to be supervising, the only problem was that the force of his jump half propelled him forward and half propelled the raft back behind him, making an already-poor decision to jump, much more difficult. I mean, it wasn't Mr. Muscalini taking flight. Mr. Gifford is a science geek, like me. Jumping from raft to raft while on a rocky river was not exactly our thing.

Instead of landing dead center in our raft, as he appeared to be aiming for, he came up seriously short, his forearms only barely able to make it inside the raft. Worse still, the force of his landing bounced the unconscious Mrs.

Funderbunk clear out of the raft. She soared through the air, still unconscious, as the straps from her life vest flapped in the breeze. It was going to end poorly, but at least she looked peaceful in that moment. We all just watched helplessly, as Mrs. Funderbunk splashed into the rancid river water and disappeared.

We all screamed, but Mrs. Funderbunk's head and shoulders bobbed up and out of the water, the life vest buoying her. The cold and foul water that most definitely went up her broken nose woke her from her unconsciousness.

Mr. Gifford let go of our raft, slipping fully into the water, and swam over to Mrs. Funderbunk. I held out my bloody paddle to try to help them, but we were moving too quickly down the river. As crazy as the situation was, Mr. Gifford never looked so happy in his life. Mrs. Funderbunk clung to him like her life depended on it, which it kind-of did. She wasn't nearly as happy, though. Her face was ghost white, except for the black streaks of mascara down her face, a result of tears and rotten river water.

Mr. Gifford shrieked excitedly, "Madeline! What an adventure!"

"Adventure? This is a tragedy! Worse than MacBeth!"

All of us unsupervised kids stared behind us in shock, as we continued float away from Mr. Gifford and Mrs. Funderbunk. We didn't realize that we should be looking where we were headed. Things were about to get even more interesting.

6

The rain from the storm was wreaking havoc on the river and on our less-than-experienced rafting crew. Rocks were disappearing from the surface and we were accelerating down the river, which was a bad combination. Nobody could control their rafts. The raft that Mr. Gifford had previously been supervising, with Randy and my brother, was spinning in circles, heading toward rocks. Mr. Muscalini, Ben, Sammie, Luke, and Dayna were also heading in that direction, against the will and biceps of Mr. Muscalini.

Some kids were screaming. Others had given up trying to paddle and were just holding on to the ropes around the edge of the raft, their knuckles whiter than their ghost-like faces. Mr. Muscalini looked around at the chaos and started blowing his whistle. I'm not entirely sure why. Maybe he was hoping it would all stop. Maybe he was calling a penalty on the weather, I don't know.

Even Colt was having difficulty. I thought he would be on a surf board or something, carving up waves, but he was paddling like a savage and yelling, "Stay left around the bank! Everybody stay left!"

"We gotta get left!" I yelled.

"There are rocks to the left," Sophie countered.

We were all seemingly rowing in different directions or maybe the river was running so fast that we didn't have the strength to overpower it and change directions. I rowed harder and faster, but the more effort I put in the less we achieved. I felt frustrated and helpless as the storm beat down on us and the river tossed us around. I wasn't sure if it was rain or buckets of sweat, but I was drenched and at my wits end.

Without warning, I was clobbered in the back of the head with what I can only assume was a paddle, even though nobody apologized. So rude. Pain seared through my head. Tears welled up in my eyes. The force of the blow not only hurt like heck, but it knocked me off my seat and crippled my will to continue. I crashed into the center of the raft onto a pile of less-than-soft water jugs. Why couldn't it have been the cushy tents? So unfair.

Sophie called out for me. "Austin! Are you okay? Austin! We need you!"

My vision was blurry. It may have been the hit to the back of my head or the monsoon. I didn't want to move. I just wanted to snuggle with a big water jug and forget every-thing that was happening. I didn't move as we smashed into something and spun around. I just wanted to be home with my parents, maybe even my brother.

Speaking of my brother, I heard him yell, "Where's Austin?" He sounded concerned, which was a first.

Sophie yelled, "He passed out!"

I would have preferred if she said I was unconscious rather than passed out.

Our rafts must have bumped into each other, because I heard Randy say, "Aww, look! Davenfart is sleeping like a baby!"

I tried not to react, but I was getting angry at all the digs he gave me. I hated the guy. I sat up and rubbed my face. "I think someone crushed my skull. How did I survive such a vicious blow?" I wasn't sure if it was too much.

Before Randy could make a snide comment, their raft crashed into another set of rocks. We followed quickly and bounced off their raft. Randy used his paddle to push us off him, which pushed us back into the middle of the river, clear of the rocks, but also spun us around. We floated down the river, most of us backwards, based on where we were sitting around the round raft.

The rain continued to pour down on us. It was relentless. We smashed into Mr. Muscalini's raft. Ditzy Dayna called to Sophie, "How do my bangs look? I'm so glad I brought that hair dryer!"

"Shut up and paddle!" Sophie yelled.

"Your bangs look lovely," Luke said.

"You never tell me the truth!" Dayna said.

Luke rolled his eyes. I couldn't believe they were arguing about her bangs while we were clinging to life.

"Take the left fork!" Colt yelled to everyone.

"I'm not even hungry," Dayna said.

"He means the left fork of the river! It splits up ahead!" Ben yelled.

I looked up toward the fork. Most of the group was in a decent position to follow Colt to the left, but my expert crew somehow was not.

"Paddles on the right. Hard!" I yelled.

"Double time!" Sophie added.

"Triple time!" Just Charles said.

"My arms are burning!" Cheryl said.

The right fork of the river pulled us harder than we could paddle away from it. I looked toward our goal, knowing full well there was no way we were going to make it. Colt and the bulk of the group disappeared down the left fork of Rotten River. I didn't know what to do.

"We're going the wrong way!" Just Charles yelled.

"Thanks for the update," I said, sarcastically.

We watched in vain as the river swept us in the opposite direction from the rest of the eighth-grade class, teachers, and most of the food. At least we would have company. Catching up to us were Mr. Muscalini and crew, along with Randy, Derek, and their crew.

"Let's go, team! We can make it!" Mr. Muscalini said. I at least admired his confidence, misguided as it was.

The river had other plans. It swept us down the right fork of the river with a mighty force.

Mr. Muscalini's crew bounced off a rock, water spraying my already-soaked friends.

Ditzy Dayna yelled, "Wheeeee!" like we were on a theme park ride that could be stopped at any moment by the push of a button.

We hit the same rock right behind them. I clunked heads with Sophie.

"You okay?" I asked.

"Never better!" Sophie yelled, sarcastically.

I looked over to Mr. Muscalini. For the first time since I'd known him, fear registered in his eyes. I looked at their raft and it appeared to be losing air.

Mr. Muscalini confirmed my suspicion. "We're gonna sink!"

"The rocks must've popped their raft!" I yelled.

Mr. Muscalini's voice boomed. "We're going down!

Gordo! You're the captain. You have to go down with the ship!"

Ben yelled, "What? It's a raft! And why am I the captain?"

"The crew voted. Sorry! You gotta do it!" Mr. Muscalini said.

I looked at Ben's face and I could tell what he was thinking. Ahhhh, farts! It was my line, but the situation definitely called for it.

7

We continued on down the river, slowly catching up to Mr. Muscalini, Ben, and the rest of their crew. Their raft was about half full and on the brink of taking on water.

"We have to save them!" Sophie yelled.

"Once the water gets over the side of the raft, it's gonna sink quick!" I yelled. I thought about Mr. Gifford for a quick second. I'm sure he would've given Mr. Muscalini a lesson on buoyancy had he still been with us. I worried about what happened to him.

"How do we save them?" Just Charles said.

"I think we have to take them with us," Cheryl said.

"They might sink us!" Just Charles yelled.

I said, "We have to try. Everybody row on the left side!"

"There!" Sophie yelled to Mr. Muscalini's crew while pointing at a downed tree, jutting out into the river. "Get to safety there! We'll pick you up!"

I admired her confidence in our rowing prowess, but I thought it might be a little aggressive. Or a lot. But we rowed like crazy and slowly made our way over. Thankfully, the sinking crew had hold of the tree. They were all climbing onto it, unstable as it was, because their raft was slowly disappearing.

We continued to make our way toward them, but it seemed like a long shot.

"We're not gonna make it!" I yelled.

"We have to!" Sophie countered.

Our crew continued rowing. We were rapidly approaching the downed tree, but we were about ten feet to the left, which meant clear sailing down the river and leaving our friends behind, stranded on a tree limb with no food and no way to contact anyone.

I looked back from my Olympic rowing effort to find Just Charles not rowing at all!

"Charles- what are you doing?" I yelled.

"We need to row!" Sophie said, echoing my thoughts.

He ignored me, as I stared at him, quickly realizing that no one was rowing. I turned back around and continued rowing like a beast.

Cheryl yelled, "You've had rain ponchos in there the whole time?"

Just Charles stammered, "I...I didn't remember! I packed so much stuff!"

"What are you even doing?" Cheryl asked, annoyed.

I looked back again. Just Charles emerged with a coiled up rope. "Just get close enough so that I can throw this to them!"

Charles readied himself with the rope, as we made our final approach.

"So, you want me to bump into them?" I asked.

"Very funny! Just a little bit closer!"

We all rowed like crazy while Just Charles steadied himself in the center of the raft. Time was slipping by quickly. I looked back to see what the heck he was doing. I wasn't entirely sure. He was checking the wind then stretching out his back, and then psyching himself up with a few smacks to his own face.

"I'm gonna smack you myself if you don't throw that rope!" Cheryl yelled. Lovingly, of course.

The raft-wrecked crew looked on in anticipation. Mr. Muscalini yelled, "Toss the rope, Zaino! And for God's sake don't throw it like a girl. You know, like every other time!"

"I won't let you down, sir!"

"I'm not counting on it, but just use your hips!" Mr. Muscalini said.

"Hips. Got it!" Just Charles wound up, rotated his hips, and let the rope fly.

It was a beautiful shot, better than any rope throwing I'd ever seen, and I've seen a lot of rope throwing in my days. It soared through the air like a rope frisbee. There was just one problem. He didn't actually hold onto the end of the rope, so the entire coil landed a foot in front of Mr. Muscalini with a splash.

"Nice throw! Now, what do we do with it?" Dayna asked.

"Throw it back!" I yelled.

"They're playing catch while we're stranded here?" Ditzy Dayna asked. "That seems wrong."

"Quick, before they're out of range!" Ben yelled.

Mr. Muscalini grabbed hold of the end of the rope in one hand, rotated his hips, and launched the rope with warp speed. I think it may have broken the sound barrier. The slack of the rope disappeared, causing the rest of the rope to uncoil as it made its way toward us.

"It's not gonna make it!" Just Charles yelled.

The rope landed in the water right next to us. I

wondered if it would disintegrate in the Rotten River water. But thankfully, it held together.

Before I could do anything, Sophie jumped into the water while holding onto the rope that ringed around the raft. She grabbed the rope with her empty hand and connected us to the crew on the downed tree. Her arms stretched as far as they could, the force of the river pulling against her.

"Help her!" I yelled to no one in particular.

Cheryl grabbed Sophie's arm and tried to pull her back into the raft. She didn't succeed, but we gained some ground in getting closer to the other group.

Mr. Muscalini started pulling us in by the rope.

"My hand is slipping! I don't know how much longer I'll be able to hold on!" Sophie yelled.

I had an idea. I was just about to say it when Cheryl beat me to it, yelling, "Let go of the raft and we'll hold your vest!"

I felt helpless. I didn't know what to do. I scooted over to the rest of the group and tried to grab on to Sophie's vest, but Cheryl and Just Charles were already holding on, and I couldn't reach.

Sophie pulled us closer, hand over hand, inch by inch. She was grunting and groaning. If she was somebody else and not my beautiful girlfriend, I'd question why there were so many air bubbles coming up from underneath the water.

The raftwrecked crew cheered her on. Mr. Muscalini continued to pull from his end and yelled, "You go, girl!"

Ditzy Dayna said, "This is so exciting! What a great trip."

Finally, a swarm of hands grabbed onto our raft, pinning us to the side of the downed tree. Mr. Muscalini reached over and picked up Sophie with both hands by grasping her life vest. He placed her into the raft.

"Thank you," she said, gasping for air.

"Are you okay?" I asked, rubbing her back.

"I'll be fine," she said. I couldn't tell if she was annoyed or if I was just self conscious for being helpless. Again.

Everybody piled into the raft. We rode a little low, but it was better than being stranded. Nobody said much of anything. I think we were all exhausted and a little bit scared. We had been separated from our group, not to mention would be supervised by Mr. Muscalini.

Eventually, we made it to a small dock that led up to an open space, most likely for campers, that also happened to contain Randy, Regan, Derek, Jayden, and Nick. While I normally had no interest in seeing them anywhere, I was at least glad that we had reconnected with them, being that we were the only three groups that had gotten separated from the rest of the tour. And even better, the rain had stopped.

Mr. Muscalini jumped out of the raft, landing knee deep in the water, and pulled the raft to the river bank. We jumped out one by one. Mr. Muscalini looked up and pointed. "Hey, look. There's our raft."

The old raft seemingly had only a few molecules of air left in it as it floated by. It let out a squeaker of a fart and then sunk, disappearing beneath the stinky surface.

Ditzy Dayna shook her head. "We had some good times in that raft."

Luke looked at her like she was crazy, which was absolutely true, and said, "We had it for like two minutes and it nearly killed us."

"Yeah, but besides that, it was okay."

Randy added to the enjoyment of the day. "Nice work, Baby Fart!" he said with a fake smile and thumbs up, which turned into an 'L' on his forehead.

I agreed with him for once. I didn't do anything to help my team, except for a bunch of rowing that did next to nothing against the current of the river. Not to mention, my rowing started the chain reaction that led to Mr. Gifford and Mrs. Funderbunk disappearing.

"Don't worry about him," Sophie said.

"He's right. I am a loser," I said, turning my back on them.

Mr. Muscalini looked at Gordo and shook his head, disapprovingly, seemingly still upset that Gordo didn't go down with the raft.

"What's the matter, sir?" Ben asked.

"Warblemacher would've gone down with that raft."

"Yeah, I 'm pretty certain he would not have," I said, grumpily.

Mr. Muscalini looked at me and said, "Gordo might've failed us all, but you have an opportunity to step up and take charge."

I just nodded, not agreeing whatsoever.

Mr. Muscalini said, "Unpack. Let's dry this stuff out, eat some lunch, and figure out how to regroup."

We emptied the two remaining rafts, carrying our equipment and rations up to a grassy area above the river bank.

Luke, Just Charles, and I grabbed water jugs off the rafts.

"Is that all of it?" Mr. Muscalini asked, holding a map in his hands.

"Yep," I said.

"Secure the rafts and then Zaino, Davenport- help me figure out this map," Mr. Muscalini said, turning it upside down, trying to figure out where the heck we were, and seemingly not doing a very good job of it.

I nodded to Ben and said, "Secure the raft while I look at the map."

Ben said, "Luke, secure the raft while I look at the map with Austin."

Luke said something, but I was too busy concentrating on the map. I thought it could be an area where I could help. I am a genius, after all.

"What the-" Randy yelled. "Idiots!"

I looked up from the map to see our two rafts floating away.

"Where are they going?" Dayna asked.

"They're goin' bye, bye. And we're in serious trouble," Regan said. "Great work, as always. Nerds."

Mr. Muscalini took a deep breath, attempting to compose himself. "I told you to secure them, Davenport!"

"I told Ben to secure them," I said, staring at Ben.

"Gordo? What did you do?" Mr. Muscalini barked.

"I told Luke to secure the rafts."

We all looked at Luke.

"Yeah, I told somebody to secure the raft."

"Who?" I asked.

"You," Luke said, nodding to me.

"You were the last one off the raft," Ben said.

I huffed. "I told Ben. He told you. Why would you tell me?"

"Everybody was telling everybody else what to do!"

"Nice work, Luke," I said.

"Oops?"

"Oops?" I asked.

"Ahhh, farts?" Luke questioned with a shrug.

We stopped arguing as we realized that everybody was staring at us with eye daggers. We were doomed.

8

The death stares eventually died down. I looked at the map with Mr. Muscalini and Just Charles while the rest of the crew paced around anxiously. Even Randy looked a little bit worried. But despite the monsoon-like weather, his hair still looked fantastic. I made it my mission to touch his hair before the trip was over so that I could find out if it was real or some crazy wig.

I pointed to the map and said, "This is where they're camping tonight. But we're never gonna catch up to them without rafts. We should just make our way down this fork of the river until we find civilization and can contact the tour company."

Mr. Muscalini was barely paying attention. "Are you sure this is the right map?"

"That sounds like a dumb idea, Davenfart," Randy said.

"You didn't even hear it," I said, rolling my eyes.

"Still, I know it was dumb."

I shook my head and concentrated on the map.

"We have no rafts and we're miles from our checkpoint. This is bad," I said.

Just Charles countered, "They'll come get us. They have to, right?"

"We can't count on that," I said.

Mr. Muscalini looked up from the map and shrugged. "Don't worry, kids. I was a scout when I was your age."

"So, what do we do?" Regan asked.

Mr. Muscalini said, "Work together as a team. Unless they're weak and then we leave them behind. Sometimes, you gotta cut your losses."

Ben, perhaps believing that Mr. Muscalini was talking about him, said, "Umm, sir? This isn't the Marines. It's a middle school class trip."

In all fairness to Ben, he could've meant me or Just Charles. Or all of us. We weren't exactly built for wilderness survival. We were barely surviving middle school on a daily basis.

Mr. Muscalini looked at his watch. "It's cardio workout time!"

I nodded. "Yeah, that's the best option we've got. We're gonna have to hike south and eventually cut over to the other fork and see if we can meet up with the rest of the group." I looked over at Mr. Muscalini who was in the midst of doing jumping jacks.

Mr. Muscalini stopped in mid jack and said, "Oh, right. Yeah, that's what I meant."

"Do you think Mrs. Funderbunk and Mr. Gifford are alright?" Cheryl asked Mr. Muscalini.

"Probably not, Miss Van Snoogle-Something," he said.

I tried not to cry. I think most of us, with the exception of the heartless couple, Randy and Regan, were all trying not to cry.

"Why the long faces? The game's not over. Yeah, we're down, but we're not out. Gifford may be fish food, but sometimes you have to take one for the team." It was not one of his best motivational speeches, but still, he continued, "We need to stick together as a team. We need to push through the obstacles that we face. We might not all make it out of here alive."

Randy chimed in. "I'm still taking bets that Davenfart gets eaten by a bear."

Mr. Muscalini nodded in agreement. "I could see that happening. So, now that you're all pumped up, let's hit the trails!"

We distributed the tents and food to everyone in the group, except for Just Charles, who still had more goods than the rest of us combined. Mr. Muscalini used the rope to string six water jugs together through the handles, and tied them to his backpack.

"Isn't that going to hurt your back?" Sammie asked.

Mr. Muscalini said, "This? Piece of cake. Although, I never actually eat cake. When I was eight, my father made me go to school with a weighted vest."

"That's weird, sir," I said, as we started walking.

"It had its benefits. Except when I wore one in high school and had really long hair and a beard. Security thought I was trying to blow up the school."

"What happened?" Sophie asked.

"They called the cops. My parents came. My dad talked all the police into training with weighted vests."

"They called the cops," I said, excitedly.

"Mr. Muscalini said, "It wasn't a good thing, Davenport. It could've cost me my scholarship."

"No, I wasn't talking about that. Charles, the burner phone!"

Just Charles' eyes bulged.

If we weren't in such a bad spot, I would've laughed. I said, "Dude, Mr. Muscalini is not gonna rat you out for having a cell phone when our lives depend on it."

"Dude!" Just Charles said. He didn't trust Mr. Muscalini farther than he could throw him, which was not at all.

"Zaino, if you have a phone, I'll let you skip one gym class a week for the rest of the year," Mr. Muscalini said.

"Oh, my God! My life finally has meaning!" Just Charles said.

"Let's not get carried away, here," Mr. Muscalini said.

Just Charles dropped his pack like a ton of bricks, which would probably be lighter than what he actually had in his pack. He rummaged through his clothes and eventually pulled out a wad of socks, stuffed into each other.

While he searched for the phone, I checked out the rest of his bag. "You got any duct tape in here?"

"Nah. Didn't bring any," Just Charles said, not looking up.

I eyed a dozen or more bungee cords. "What do you need so many bungee cords for?"

"You can never have enough bungee cords. They're the better cousin of duct tape. And if anybody knows the power of duct tape it's you," Just Charles said, referring to the many times I had been duct taped during my adventures in high school science.

"Which is why it's a crime that you didn't bring any," I countered.

Just Charles ignored me and thrust his hand into the socks and slid a small cellphone out of the sock.

"He's gonna get us out of here," Regan said, excitedly.

"He's a hero!" Ben celebrated.

Just Charles pressed the power button. The phone lit up. I peered over his shoulder. The two of us stared at the phone, waiting for the cellular bars to appear. We waited. And waited. And waited.

My shoulders slumped. "There's no signal here."

The celebratory mood soured quickly. Mr. Muscalini even lost his cool, kicking a tree limb. He almost uprooted it, but he also hopped around holding his foot. He said, "Dang it! My pinky toe!"

"We're gonna die out here," Jayden said.

"Bears are gonna eat all of us," Derek added.

Randy responded, "I'll still win my bet."

"That's what you care about? Winning your bet when you're dead?" Sophie asked, annoyed.

Mr. Muscalini stopped hopping around. He cleared his throat. "Sorry about that back there. Even though I may lose that toe, we have to move on. We can try the phone down the river. Let's move out!"

We hit the hiking trail. Of course, all the nerds trailed in the back. Just Charles was by far the worst. Not only was he the worst athlete of all of us, he also had asthma, and like fifty pounds of camping gear, home goods, and snacks.

It was dead quiet. Nobody said anything. All we heard was the river running, the crunching of twigs and leaves, and the huffing and puffing of nerds. We were depressed, and weighed down with physical and emotional baggage.

After only about ten minutes, Just Charles called out to us from about thirty feet back, "I need a break!"

"We've got...miles to...go!" I yelled back in between deep breaths.

"Let's go, back there!" Mr. Muscalini yelled. "Bring up the rear!"

"What did he say?" Just Charles asked.

"He said, 'you're the butt of the group and to get your butt moving!" I yelled back.

Just Charles whined, "I don't want to be the stinky butt..."

We continued on for a while, the windy path of the river guiding us to our destination. I lumbered up to the rest of the group, dropped my pack on the ground, and collapsed. I was exhausted, but it was a self-directed collapse. I don't want you to get too worried about me.

Just Charles eventually arrived. His pack nearly dented the ground. It probably woke every animal in a quarter mile with the giant clank that reverberated through the woods.

"I need water," Just Charles said. He took out his canteen and nearly downed the whole thing. It was a full on chug with gulping and splashing.

"They're disgusting creatures, aren't they?" Regan asked.

I looked at Just Charles' pack. "What do you have in here?" I started to go through it. Ben joined me.

"Is that a lava lamp? And what do you have Apple Cider Vinegar for?" Ben asked.

Just Charles responded defensively, "It soothes my sore throat. Plus I like it on salads."

I rolled my eyes. "Who's eating salads here?"

"Good point," Just Charles said.

I pulled out the next wacky item. "What the heck do you need a hulk action figure for?"

"Put that away!"

Ben pulled out a can of beans. "We have beans, but I haven't actually seen a can opener. Do you have one?"

"Probably. Maybe. I'm not really sure."

At that moment, we all heard something crackle behind a line of bushes. We froze for a moment, but didn't hear anything.

"It's probably the bear coming to eat Davenfart," Randy

said to laughter. "The bear's coming to get you," he said, spookily. "And it's gonna make me rich."

"How much money could you possibly make if I got eaten by a bear?"

"About $200."

"That's just wrong," Sophie said.

Sammie asked, "Does anybody hear that buzzing?"

"It's just the hum from the river," Mr. Muscalini said, confidently.

Luke said, "Who cares about bears eating kids. I want a spider bite. I want to be Spider Man."

Sophie rolled her eyes. "It doesn't work that way."

"This trip stinks," Luke said. I was surprised that after all we had been through, he thought it stunk because he didn't become Spider Man, like the rest of our trip was just awesome.

Cheryl pointed above the bushes. Her mouth dropped open. "What about bees?"

I looked up to see a swarm of angry bees heading toward us.

"Run!" Mr. Muscalini yelled.

9

We all took off running in every direction. Well, except directly toward the bees. It was surprising, really. I thought that at the very least, Ditzy Dayna might want to pet them.

Sophie grabbed my hand and pulled me down the side of the river bank. We slid down, our feet stopping just at the water's edge, and leaned up against the bank. Mr. Muscalini, Nick, and Jayden all plunged into the river. There was no way I was going in there. We were low enough that the bees would fly over us, but they didn't even appear to follow us.

We sat in silence for a few minutes, not sure where the bees or the rest of our crew went.

Regan broke the silence, shrieking, "My baby! What have they done to you?"

We all rushed back up the river bank and over to the crew that had reassembled at our break spot.

"What happened?" Cheryl asked, concerned.

The crew had surrounded Randy. Based on Regan's dramatics, I had expected him to emerge from the crowd, looking like the Hunchback of Notre Dame. Unfortunately, that was not the case.

"I'll be fine," he said, breaking away from the group.

I looked at Randy in shock. He must have gotten stung by the bees on his face. It was swollen. But not the distorted swollen kind. Somehow it made him better looking. His face looked fuller. More manly. It wasn't fair.

Mr. Muscalini stepped forward, dripping wet from the river jump. He said, "Warblemacher, you okay?"

Randy nodded.

"Good. Thanks for taking one for the team. God forbid those bees got to my biceps. These monsters would've torn right through my sleeves. They're tight enough as it is." He smiled at his biceps for a moment and then said, "We've got to get to higher ground to make camp."

"Why can't we camp by the river?" Derek asked.

Mr. Muscalini said, "If a storm hits, we don't want to be downhill or too close to the water. Gather your stuff. The whistle blows in five."

After the break, we climbed up a hill, huffing and puffing, until we came to a flat trail. We rested for a minute, waiting for Just Charles to join us. Eventually, he made it.

"Did you feel that?" Sophie asked.

I frowned. "Feel what?"

"The ground move. And what's that rumbling?"

"I think Mr. Muscalini farted," I said.

Sophie shook her head. "No, it was more than that."

Beneath me, I felt the ground move "I felt that," I said.

Sophie pulled me around to look up the hill. She was stunned into silence. I did a double take. My eyes widened, as I took in the scene. There was mud. A lot of it. And it was heading right for us like an avalanche.

"Mudslide!" Derek yelled.

It was as if a ginormous chocolate milkshake tipped over and was running down the hill. Although probably not as tasty.

I almost made some mud in my pants, but was too busy with the ground beneath us giving out.

"Ahhh, farts!" I yelled.

My feet slid out from under me. We were all on our butts, sliding down the side of the hill. At first, it was kind of fun. Like a dirty water slide, but then we started bouncing off of trees and bushes, which was less than fun. After a few hits to the head, I think I was a bit punch drunk. I looked over to see Randy surfing the mudslide like he was carving up an ocean wave. I did a double take and saw a squirrel surfing a mud wave on top of a piece of tree bark. I didn't know what was going on. `

I was jolted back to reality when I heard Ben yell, "Hold hands!"

Luke yelled back, "I don't want to hold hands with you!"

What an idiot. I looked over to see Sophie sliding down beside me. I leaned over and reached out my hand for her. She reached for mine. Our fingers touched as we bumped along. But we couldn't quite get a hold of each other. I leaned closer toward her, mud running and splattering every which way around me. I could've used my science goggles. I wondered if Just Charles had any in his backpack. He probably left them at home and took a shoe horn and pencil sharpener instead.

Before I could ask him, Sophie screamed, "Look out!"

I looked down the hill ahead of me and saw Ben and Sammie hit a bump and catapult into the air. I looked around for a tree or root to grab, but I couldn't find anything. I dug my heels into the mud, but I barely slowed. I hit the bump at close to full speed and surged into the air. For a brief second, it was euphoric. I soared into the air like a bird. Caught in the moment, I yelled out, "I can fly!" But then I quickly remembered the important science lesson on gravity. People can't fly. I plummeted to the muddy ground with what I'm sure was a manly scream, and disappeared into a pool of mud, face first.

I could feel mud piling up on top of me, weighing me down. I half-climbed, half-swam to the top. I held my breath, the weight getting heavier and heavier. I thrust my fist up through the mud and it found open air. Energized, I pushed my body higher, and found enough air to keep me going. I climbed onto a more stable bit of ground to avoid drowning in mud. But the mud was still running. I turned my back on it and just tried to hold my ground, protecting my face with my arms to create an unobstructed air tunnel. It worked well enough, but I did inhale a few mud pies. Not sure why kids eat those. It was disgusting. It certainly didn't taste like a giant chocolate shake.

When the mud run stopped, I spit out a mouthful of the tasty stuff, took a nice big breath of mud-free air, and wiped the, you guessed it, mud, from my eyes. I immediately wished I hadn't. My heart pounded like a drum. I didn't know what to do. There was certainly mud in my pants and some of it was likely self-induced. Staring down at me were three giant brown bears, standing on their hind legs. It was like Goldilocks, but instead of a breakfast of porridge on the menu, I was the breakfast.

I let out my best battle cry, which for some reason came out like a shrieking baby. Maybe the mud in my brain forgot it was supposed to be a battle cry and not just a regular cry.

But I had bigger issues than to try to figure that out. I was about to become people porridge and die a painful death. And that meant Randy would win the bet. Oh, and I would be dead. So there's that.

10

The bears stared down at me, expressionless. I didn't know what to do. I yelled out, "I don't have any porridge, so please don't eat me!"

I heard Randy laugh and say, "Davenfart, you're Goldilocks! That's the funniest thing I've ever seen."

I was confused. I didn't know why he was so chill about three bears. Maybe it was because they were about to eat me and he was gonna be $200 richer. But then the bears starting laughing and wiped their faces. Mud fell to the ground in a clump. The brown bears were not actually bears, but Mr. Muscalini, Nick, and Derek.

I took a deep breath and exhaled, grateful that they were not going to eat me.

"Dang it," Randy said. "I was gonna buy my girl something pretty if Davenfart kicked the bucket."

"Aww, you're so sweet," Regan said.

"And that makes you, baby bear, Davenport," Randy said to Derek.

Derek didn't say anything, but wiped a gob of mud from his shoulder and rocketed it toward Randy's head. Randy dodged the incoming mud ball. It exploded on the tree behind him, spraying everyone with mud. Nobody really cared, because we were already all sprayed with mud.

I looked over at Randy. He had a few spots with mud on him, but had like 2% of what everyone else had. He shook out his hair. Mud splattered on the rest of us and his golden locks were spotless, like he had just stepped out of a shampoo commercial.

"Why do you call him Davenport and me Davenfart?" I asked.

"Because I don't hate him."

Sophie said, "Just ignore him."

"I do, but it doesn't seem to deter him, does it?"

"Nope," Sophie said.

I looked around and scanned the crowd. "Where's Sammie?" I was taken aback by some random dude standing next to me. "And who the heck are you?" I asked, checking out the dude's mustache. It was thick and full. The kind of mustache a middle schooler dreams of.

"It's me, idiot!" Sammie said, wiping the mud from her face, taking the glorious 'stache with it.

Cheryl wiped her face and said, "This is disgusting."

"Simmer down," Mr. Muscalini said. "Who doesn't love a good mud bath? I just need two cucumber slices for my eyes. Zaino? You got cucumbers in your pack?"

"Umm, no, sir."

Mr. Muscalini's shoulders slumped. "Unbelievable." It was kind of odd that he would be upset that Just Charles didn't have a cucumber, because who would pack a cucumber for a camping trip? That being said, he had so many other useless things in his pack, it was entirely possible that he had a host of vegetables.

"I may have a rutabaga or a jar of pickles," Just Charles

said. He looked through his bag. "Nope. Must've left that at home."

Ben said, "I think I swallowed seventeen pounds of mud." He spit out some on the ground.

"That's disgusting," Dayna said.

Luke said, "Yeah, the Babybot poop tasted better."

Randy said, "I, for one, feel refreshed. That ride was exhilarating. It reminded me of that triple black diamond I did the first day I tried snowboarding."

Mr. Muscalini said, "Quit your complaining, everyone. The mineral content in this mud is off the charts. Anybody got a multi-vitamin in their bag?"

"No, sir," Just Charles said.

"Then start eating some mud. We gotta keep our micros up."

"What the heck is a micro?" Nick asked.

"I'm not eating mud," Regan said, snottily.

I didn't blame her for not wanting to eat mud, but I almost downed a handful just to spite her. I almost hated her as much as I hated Randy. Almost.

Ben helped me to my feet. My legs were a little wobbly. It felt like the ground was still moving. I guessed it was normal after a mudslide.

"What's the matter?" Sophie asked.

"I looked like an idiot back there," I said.

"In fairness, don't you always look like an idiot?" Derek chimed in.

"Not now, Derek," I said, annoyed.

Ben joined the conversation, "Dude, you're supposed to be scared of a bear. Everyone is."

"Yeah, but you can be scared and still do the right thing. I shrieked like a baby."

"I thought that's what you're supposed to do," Sophie said.

I shook my head. "You're supposed to act all crazy and make it scared of you."

"Everybody here?" Mr. Muscalini asked. "Let's do an attendance check." He patted his shirt and pants pockets. Mud splattered everywhere. "I don't seem to have my attendance sheet." He scanned the group. "How many are we supposed to be?"

Everybody shrugged.

"Notice anyone missing?" Mr. Muscalini asked. Nobody said anything. "All right. That's good enough for me."

My legs were still wobbly. I shook them out, trying to get them back to normal, as we walked down to a hiking trail.

Sophie asked, "How does my hair look?" She was fussing with it.

I didn't know what to say. "Different." Her brown curls were defying gravity and heading in every direction.

"You look like Medusa, right, Austin?" Ditzy Dayna said, like it was a good thing to look like a woman with live, venomous snakes in her hair.

"Umm, not really seeing it. No," I lied. I wanted to survive the trip.

Sammie asked, "What's that noise?"

"It just sounds like thunder in the distance," Ben said.

"Thunder doesn't shake the ground," Cheryl said.

"I feel that, too," I said.

Luke asked, "Is it another mudslide? An earthquake?"

Just Charles was, of course, in the back of the group, on account of his oversized pack and undersized muscles, just around the bend behind Sophie and me. I looked back toward him when I heard him screaming. I couldn't understand what he was saying, but it was clear that he was running away from something. Fast. Well, faster than I'd ever seen him run.

"What's going on?" Sophie asked.

Just Charles blew right past us, his pack bouncing and clanking with each step. "Run! It's a stampede!"

"Huh?" I asked, as Just Charles left us in the dust.

Sophie grabbed my wrist and pulled me forward. We took off behind Just Charles. It was better to run and it be nothing than walk and get stampeded.

I looked over my shoulder as we ran. It was hard to see beyond my back pack, but I eventually got a clear shot behind me. My eyes nearly exploded out of my head, I was so surprised. "Moose! It's a moose stampede!" I yelled.

Our entire group was now in a full out sprint, heading down a tree-lined hiking path.

I was only a few feet behind Just Charles, Ben, and Sammie.

Just Charles called out over his shoulder, "I think it's meese!"

"What?" I asked, huffing and puffing.

"The plural of moose is meese!"

I called back, "Thanks, I'm sure I'll use that when I'm dead from the moose stampede!"

"You could've just used it!"

"Dang it!" I yelled.

I didn't actually think he was right, but I wasn't going to argue the point. I had bigger problems to worry about. I had a herd of moose/meese that stretched eight feet wide rumbling toward my butt like I was running with the bulls in Pamplona, Spain. Note to self: Don't ever run with the bulls in Pamplona, Spain.

I engaged my lightning quick speed and took off down the path, the moose gaining on me. I looked ahead and saw nothing but a dense wall of trees lining the path. I wondered if I would get more respect if I survived a moose stampede and had a hundred hoof prints tattooed on my butt and elsewhere. I was pretty certain that moose stampede survivors would have a serious amount of street cred.

I was also pretty certain that there weren't actually any moose stampede survivors. And the likelihood of me and my nerd crew being the first survivors had a negative probability. I was going to be flattened like a pancake, pounded into the mud for all eternity.

I dodged giant puddles and ducked under vines that hung down from the trees overhead. And not always doing a great job of dodging or ducking. My left foot was soaking wet and I think I had twelve leaves up my nose. It could've been thirteen. I wasn't counting. The footsteps were getting louder. I looked back as I ran to find a moose staring back at me. His hot, smelly breath kind-of reminded me of the beef stew back at the school cafeteria. I never wanted to be back there so badly in my life, because I was about to be trampled to death. I figured poison by beef stew would be a less painful way to go. Although, maybe not by much.

11

I huffed down the path, the herd's pounding footsteps growing. Smelly Breath, which is what I named the moose on my tail, kept nudging me with his snout. It was getting harder and harder. If he got any closer, he might give me a flat tire or bump me too far forward that I'd face plant and then it would be game over for Austin. My family would easily replace me with my new butt-chinned sister, but I wasn't ready to go just yet.

I looked ahead to find an opening in the path. My crew had disappeared ahead of me. My heart, on the verge of explosion, leapt in excitement that they were safe and I had a chance to join them. But my brain did some quick calculations and realized that Smelly (we were getting close, so it's my new nickname for him) and the rest of his herd were running too quickly for me to make it to safety. Smelly, seemingly not aware of my affection for him, bumped me between the shoulder blades. Hard. I nearly lost my balance forward. The only thing that kept me from getting trampled was the vines. I grabbed a handful that kept me afoot. I had to do something.

The vines! I had no choice but to go full Tarzan. By my calculations, Smelly was bumping me every four footsteps. On the fourth step, I jumped into the air and released my best Tarzan roar with my own little spin on it. "Ahhhaaaah-hhhaaaaahhhhhaaaaahhhhh, fahhhaaaahhhhaaarts!"

Moose are not really known for their timing, but Smelly's timing was impeccable. He bumped me with his snout, adding fuel to my already ferocious jump. I reached as high up as I could with both hands and grabbed a clump of vines. My momentum took my legs forward. Smelly ran beneath me, as my legs began to swing back, gravity taking hold. I let go of the vines with a yelp and squeezed my eyes shut, not wanting to watch, expecting that I would fall between a pair of moose and get trampled. Luckily enough, I felt my butt land hard on something, bounce up in the air, and then crash back down. I opened my eyes to find myself riding atop my old pal, Smelly. I squeezed my legs around him as hard as I could and wrapped my arms around his neck, as we barreled down the path.

My heart pounded. My nostrils burned. Smelly was a good moose, maybe even the best, but even the best of them stink to high heaven, especially those that live along Rotten River.

As we continued down the path, my confidence grew. Eventually, my herd made it to the clearing. My old crew waited behind trees and rocks, as Smelly and I led the herd past them. Face after face registered shock and confusion. They were moosemerized. Too corny? I'm not married to it. I was not only King of Nerd Nation. I was Master of Meese! Or was it moose? I couldn't remember. All the bouncing had jumbled my thoughts. Despite being unsure of my specific title, my confidence continued to run high, so I decided to scream it to the entire forest. "I'm the Master of Meese!"

When Smelly and the others entered the open space following the clearing, they started to slow down. At the sight of a small pond crossing our path just ahead of us,

Smelly stopped and kicked his hind legs in the air. I held on as tight as I could, but the forward momentum of the powerful moose was too much to counteract. Smelly, my former favorite moose, bucked me off his back. I flew into the air, heading to the pond with an "Aaahhhh, farts!" It was nowhere near as cool as my Tarzan roar. And the belly flop hurt.

Sophie, Ben, and Mr. Muscalini were the first of the group over to me. I stood waist deep in the pond, trying to catch my breath and hold in my tears. Belly flops aren't fun.

"Are you okay?" Sophie asked.

"I think so."

"How did you do that?" Sophie asked.

Mr. Muscalini said, "Respect, Davenport." He pounded his chest and bowed his head.

The rest of my crew surrounded me, as I waded onto the shore.

"What happened?" Ben asked.

I pushed the wet hair out of my eyes and dried my glasses on Ben's still damp shirt. It was better than my soaked one. "I was running just ahead of the herd. Smelly was bumping me."

"Who's Smelly?" Cheryl asked.

"The moose that I rode. I named him. We bonded. Well, I thought we did until he launched me into the pond. Anyway, he was about to trample me, so I jumped, grabbed a vine, and expertly mounted Smelly. You saw the rest."

"That's insane," Luke said.

"Unbelievable," Sammie added.

"Big deal. I would've landed on my feet," Randy said.

Mr. Muscalini looked around. "While we're here, we should rinse off in the pond."

"I'm not going in there," Just Charles said. "There could be brain-eating amoeba."

"There are no brain-eating amoeba in here," Nick said.

"Maybe not by you because they'd starve to death," Luke said.

"I don't get it," Nick said.

I decided to change the subject before Luke got pummeled by the biggest kid in the school. "Sir, it's going to get dark soon. Based on the map, we're not gonna catch up to them tonight. We have to set up camp before it gets too late."

Just Charles looked at the map and nodded.

"Let me look at that," Mr. Muscalini said.

Ditzy Dayna looked at the map as well. "It's not that far. It's only like an inch."

"Yeah, and that inch equates to about six miles," Just Charles said.

"That's more problematic," Mr. Muscalini said. "I have a great idea, everybody. We're not gonna catch up tonight, so let's set up camp."

I rolled my eyes at Sophie.

WE FOUND A FLAT, protected area that didn't appear to be an active moose passageway, and settled down to make camp. I worked with Ben, Just Charles, and Luke to set up our tent that we were going to share with Mr. Muscalini. I was minding my own business, staking down the tent when I felt pain searing across the back of my legs. I fell to my knees and did everything I could not to cry like a baby.

I didn't need to turn around to figure out what

happened. I knew who it was even before the high-pitched cackle echoed through the woods.

"That's it," I said through gritted teeth.

I stood up, grabbed the tent pole out of Ben's hand and faced Randy. I remembered the time I dueled him at the Renaissance Fair. You may remember that story. All I had to do was keep him out of my circle and pop some bubbles.

Randy smirked. "What are you gonna do about it, Davenfart?"

I stepped closer to Randy, readying my plastic weapon. "I'm gonna shove this up-" I stopped abruptly. I pointed behind him and yelled, "Bear!"

Randy's face lost all color. He turned around in a panic. Before he realized there weren't any bears behind him, I unleashed a monstrous blow to the small of his back with a thwack.

He let out a yelp and turned to me, a grimace on his face. It didn't stay for long. The familiar smirk was back in no time. "You're gonna regret that, Davenfart."

Randy surged forward poking and prodding me with his tent pole. I remembered my knight training and moved out and to the side, trying to keep him out of my circle, but he was too fast and I was out of sword-fighting shape. I couldn't stop the barrage of the tent pole pummeling.

"Stop it!" Sophie yelled.

"Yeah," Ben added, unhelpfully.

Mr. Muscalini emerged from the bushes and pushed his way between us. "Can't a man poop in peace?"

Randy took another shot at me, connecting with my butt, which was already sore from riding Smelly.

"Whoah. Whoah. Hold on a second. What are you doing, Warblemacher?" Mr. Muscalini asked.

At least he was going to get in trouble.

Or not. Mr. Muscalini continued, "A baseball player needs to use his hips more. Rotate them with a weight shift forward and you'll mash. Try it again. Davenport, don't block this one."

Sophie chimed in, "Don't you think you should tell them not to hit each other?"

"Oh, right. That makes sense. Knock it off. Finish setting up the tents."

I just shook my head and went back to what I was doing.

"Are you okay?" Sophie asked.

"Yep. Thanks for the help," I said.

"You sure?"

"Uh, huh."

Ben chimed in. "What do I have to do if I have to go to the bathroom?"

"Go behind a bush and pee," I said.

"It's not that kind of bathroom visit."

"Oh," I said.

"Is Max here?" Ben asked. Max was the bathroom attendant at the high school. "Please tell me he's got a portapotty station somewhere."

"Sadly, no."

"This is gonna be terrible."

Mr. Muscalini was helping the other crew set up their tent. "You're my captain, Warblemacher. Start captaining."

"Okay, sir," Randy said. "Nick, get the roof for the tent. Jayden, stake it down."

Mr. Muscalini said, "We're one team here, Randy. That means captaining everyone."

"Oh, joy," I muttered.

Randy looked over at us. "Hey, Davenfart. Go find some firewood."

"I'm not getting firewood, idiot."

Mr. Muscalini said, "Davenport, we need some firewood. Go get some."

"Okay, but because you told me to do it. Not him."

Randy smirked and used his hand to make a 'C' on his chest and then an 'L' on his forehead, pointing at me.

12

I returned with fire wood, thankful I didn't get eaten by a bear, although I was pretty sure a few people were disappointed. I dropped the fire wood in a pile at the edge of the campsite. Mr. Muscalini walked over.

"We're gonna have to chop some of this," he said.

Mr. Muscalini knelt down next to a particularly long log. He loosened his neck and took some rapid deep breaths. He lined up the ridge of his hand with the center of the log.

Just Charles stepped forward. "Umm, Mr. Muscalini, we have an axe."

Mr. Muscalini waved him off. "Nonsense. I'm a second degree blackbelt in Judo."

We all watched, not sure what was going to happen. I had seen plenty of YouTube videos of karate masters breaking boards and bricks with their hands and even heads, but I had never seen Mr. Muscalini attempt any. He was more into breaking nerd spirits and bad nutritional habits.

Mr. Muscalini raised his open hand behind his head in karate chop position. He let out a blood curdling, "Kiaaaah!"

His hand sliced through the air and connected with the wood with a thud. Mr. Muscalini grabbed his hand in pain. "Ahhh, Mommy! I broke my hand!"

"Are you okay?" Sophie rushed forward, grabbing his hand to look at it.

Mr. Muscalini whimpered. "No pain. No gain. I've got another one."

Randy stepped forward, his chest puffed out, overconfident as usual. "I'll chop the wood," he said, grabbing the axe from Just Charles. He looked at me and said, "Back up. Don't want you kids to get hurt. Well, most of you."

"Let's go get more wood," I said to Ben.

"What if there are bears out there?" he asked, afraid.

I shrugged. "Well, we'll see who runs faster."

"Wait, what?" Ben asked.

"Dude, I 'm just kidding. We'll be fine." Maybe.

We returned ten minutes later. Derek was setting the wood up for the fire while Randy was still chopping the last few pieces.

Without warning, Randy turned and threw the axe as hard as he could directly at Sammie.

"What the-" I yelled.

Sammie shrieked.

The axe tomahawked right past Sammie's leg, plunging into the ground, but not before removing a snake's head from the rest of its body.

"What's wrong with you? You could've killed her!" Ben yelled.

Randy yelled back, "It was a poisonous snake. I saved her life!"

"It's a garden snake," I said.

"It is not," Randy said, strutting toward the headless snake. That patterning means that it's a Western Mud Striker. It turns your blood to mud in fifteen minutes. No antidote."

"You're so full of it, Warblemacher," I said, with an annoyed chuckle.

"Google it, Davenfart."

I rolled my eyes. "I'm just waiting for the Wi-Fi to reset."

"There's Wi-Fi out here? I wish I had my phone," Dayna said.

Randy looked at me and said, "Don't get so upset every time I know more than you. It's gonna happen a lot. That's why I'm the captain."

"Whatever."

Mr. Muscalini interrupted, "Let's get the fire going and sing some campfire songs."

"Let's not," a bunch of us muttered in unison.

"That was pretty impressive," Sammie said to Sophie.

Sophie nodded. I nearly vomited. Ben's mouth dropped open.

"I gathered that firewood, you know," I said.

"Why does it always have to be a competition?" Sophie said.

"Whatever," I said.

Luke said, "I'm soaking wet. I can't wait to dry off by that fire."

Randy attempted to light the fire, but after a few tries, threw the lighter down on the ground. "The wood is too wet. Davenfart can't even figure out how to get dry firewood."

My blood started to boil. "It's not my fault it rained! You figure out how to get dry fire wood after a monsoon, you stupid buffoon." It's usually not a great idea to call a football player a buffoon, but it rhymed, so I went with it.

Randy stepped forward, gritting his teeth.

"Boys," Mr. Muscalini said, stepping between us, holding his broken hand. "Tensions are running high. I get it. It's been a tough day. That soggy wood was hard enough to break my hand. Thanks for that, Davenport. But we're a team."

"What?" I said to myself. "I didn't break your hand. Your terrible Judo did that."

"I'm a second degree blackbelt. I did a twelve-week course on the Internet," Mr. Muscalini said, proudly.

"What do we do about dinner?" Ben said, thankfully changing the subject.

"I've got a ton of snacks," Just Charles said.

Derek looked through the supplies. "There's some stuff we can eat in here that doesn't need to be heated up."

We all gathered around, as Derek and Just Charles handed out the food.

I loved cuisine from all over the world- Italian, Mexican,

Indian, Japanese, Chinese, and Greek. The only cuisine I hated was Cherry Avenue Middle School cafeteria food. But after that trip I had a second loathsome food group. It was a new cuisine that I didn't know existed. Soggy food. We ate soggy cookies, soggy granola bars, and soggy fruit. Who knew fruit could even *be* soggy?

After dinner, it was dark and everyone was exhausted. We didn't have a fire to sing joyous campfire songs around, so we cleaned up and got ready to turn in for the night.

I dropped Sophie off at her tent, the gentlemanly thing to do, and headed over to mine.

Randy picked up a rope. I wasn't sure if he was going to tie me up or something. He tossed it at me. I didn't flinch. It hit me in the chest and fell to the ground.

"Cat-like reflexes," Randy said, chuckling. "Mr. Muscalini said you should tie up the leftover food. You do know how to tie a knot, right?"

"Yeah, I know how to tie a knot," I said, annoyed. "But I don't take orders from you."

"They're from Mr. Muscalini," Randy said, walking away.

I looked down at the rope, kicked it for good measure, and walked away.

I sat outside on a soggy log for a few minutes before turning in to bed. Nobody said much of anything as we lay in our sleeping bags. We were either exhausted, disgusted, or angered by something or someone.

I hoped for better dreams than the nightmare we were living.

13

I was the first from my tent to get up. I quietly exited the tent. I nearly woke everyone up with my growling stomach. Apparently, soggy cookies are not that filling. It was nice just sitting on a soggy log with no one bothering me. It only lasted a few short minutes, though. People started waking up and filing out of the tents, hair flying in every direction.

Sophie exited her tent and I nearly fell over. Her curls flew in every direction and nearly didn't make it out of the tent without hitting the walls.

"What's the matter?" she asked.

"Absolutely nothing," I said. I was not going down that road.

"I'm hungry. Let's get breakfast going," Sophie said.

Randy emerged from the tent. "Davenfart, where did you tie up the food?"

Oops. "Umm, over there," I said, pointing to the area where I didn't tie up the food.

"Davenfart, you idiot!" Randy yelled.

I took a deep breath and walked over there.

"Animals ate all our food!" Randy looked at me. "Did you tie up the food, Davenfart? Or are you just incompetent?"

I looked down at the gnarled scraps on the ground. I had to think quickly. "I can't believe this," I said, stalling. "The animals must've climbed the tree and gotten to it. Amazing what those creatures can do."

"Yeah, it is," Randy said, seemingly buying my lie. "And they're so nice. Not your typical wildlife. They untied the rope and recoiled it just like it came out of the factory."

I looked down at the rope that Randy had thrown at me the night before. "Oops."

"Oops? We're all gonna starve out here because of you, Davenfart!" Randy yelled, and then bumped me out of the way.

I looked over at Sophie and Ben. Sophie took a deep breath and then walked away.

Ben mouthed, "What'd you do?"

I just shrugged. I had to salvage what I could. I followed a trail of crumbs and garbage into the woods, looking for something. Anything. And then I struck gold. My eyes widened at the site of a box of Fruit Loops. I rushed toward it and picked it up. Outside of a few loops on the ground, the box was uneaten. I guess bears and raccoons prefer oatmeal or omelettes.

"Good news!" I said, walking up to the group.

Randy interjected, "You got washed down the river in the storm?" Regan and Nick chuckled.

Sophie said, "Randy, you're such an idiot."

I ignored him. "I found a box of fruit loops. We can each have like fifty loops each."

"I don't eat anything that's not organic," Randy scoffed.

"Okay, more loops for the rest of us," I said.

I poured bowls of loops and handed them out. We all ate like savages. I'd never seen loops devoured so quickly. Even Randy looked tempted to eat some. He reached over to Regan's bowl and tried to grab one, but she smacked his hand away.

"What now?" Sophie asked.

"I was gonna go chop some wood," I said, in my manliest voice, trying to regain some credibility.

"For what? We've gotta pack up and leave," Sophie said.

"Good point," I said, sheepishly.

"Pack up camp, everyone," Randy called out.

"I hear there are cannibals around here," Luke said, shakily.

"No, there aren't," Cheryl said.

Mr. Muscalini looked at us horrified. "Be on the lookout. They don't have to already be cannibals. Even if they're thinking about being cannibals, these meaty thighs are at risk." He nodded to me. "Davenport, you lead."

"Thanks for trusting me, sir," I said with a smile.

"I meant you're the first line of defense. Those scrawny legs should repulse cannibals." Before I could respond, Mr. Muscalini bellowed, "To the rafts!"

Just Charles chimed in, "Sir, we have no rafts. They floated down the river. Without passengers."

"Oh, that's kind of a problem. We'll just hike it! Double time."

And just at that moment, the rain began to pour down on us once again.

Mr. Muscalini huffed and asked, "Just Charles, do you have any umbrellas?"

"Not at the moment, no, but I have some ponchos."

"Would've been useful before we got soaked," Cheryl said, taking one anyway.

Just Charles held the ponchos out for the girls to take. Which they did. Like savages.

It was going to be another doozy of a day. I could feel it in every fiber of my being.

14

———

Our squad headed out for another day of hiking. Despite eating most of Just Charles' snacks, his bag was still packed to the brim. We had eight miles to hike and he was going about a mile an hour.

My shoulder ached. I cursed Smelly, my former favorite moose, under my breath. My pack weighed on my back, each step reminding me of getting tossed into the pond.

"Hey, Master of Mooses-" Randy said.

I cut him off, "It's meeses. Everybody knows that."

"I'm terribly sorry. I was just going to suggest that perhaps by renouncing that title, you might not smell like a moose anymore?" "Should we call him Moosefart? The smell is spot on."

I ignored him. Nobody said much of anything for the next few miles. I checked the map here and there to make sure we didn't miss the bridge we were heading toward. It would allow us to cut across the fork in the river that we mistakenly had gone down and get us back on target to where we were supposed to end up in the rafts.

The hiking path we were on was a hundred feet or so

from the river. As the path wound down toward the river, I could see the bridge through the trees.

"The bridge!" I yelled.

There were high fives and a few cheers. With a renewed energy, we cut through weeds and brush, heading toward the bridge.

"Shouldn't the path be a little bit more worn?" I asked.

"I'm sure it's fine," Mr. Muscalini said.

We walked up to the bridge, which hung suspended a good thirty feet above the rippling, rotten water. Wood planks with wire handrails stretched over rocks that jutted from the water.

I stepped forward, "I'm not walking across that. We're gonna die on that."

Randy looked at me, disgusted. "Davenfart, fear is a disease."

Mr. Muscalini said, "Nonsense! It looks totally stable. I've been cliff diving before. This is a piece of cake. Gordo might not survive it, but the rest of us will." We stood there, staring at the rickety bridge, nobody willing to go first. "It's now or never," Mr. Muscalini said.

"Umm, I vote never," Ben said.

Mr. Muscalini ignored him. "One at a time across. DeRozan. You first."

Nick looked at the rickety bridge. "Sir, I think you should go first. You're our leader."

"It's a fair argument, but as your leader, I have a different plan. Somebody's got to test the bridge. I think it should be you."

Sophie stepped forward. "That's not right. You should go first."

Mr. Muscalini said, "I can't risk something happening to me. Who would lead you then?"

"Somehow, I think we'd be better off," Regan muttered.

"You first, then," Mr. Muscalini said to Sophie.

"No, you," she replied. It was like a bunch of kids playing the game, 'not it.'

Mr. Muscalini tried a different approach. "Okay, Warblemacher. You're the captain of the baseball team. I think you should do it. You've been talking such a big game about your leadership skills."

"I'm tired of this nonsense," Cheryl said, stepping forward. "I'll go first."

"Cheryl, no!" Just Charles said.

"I'll go first," I said. "But just a quick test." I picked up a rock and tossed it out onto the bridge a few seconds before Cheryl made it there. The rock connected with one of the wooden boards. I was no baseball prodigy, and even so, the rotten board exploded on impact, leaving a gaping hole in the bridge.

We all looked on, eyes wide.

"Now, look what you did, Davenfart!" Randy yelled.

15

We all stood around, still staring at the bridge. Most of us were still taking in the totality of what just happened. Others didn't seem to grasp it.

"Now what do we do?" Randy asked. "Davenfart messed everything up. Again."

"I just saved all our lives," I spat.

Randy wasn't giving in. "I guess that's one way to look at it."

Sophie chimed in, "Umm, it's the only way to look at it."

I looked at the map. "The next way across is another four or five miles."

"Well, then we march," Mr. Muscalini said, leading us ahead.

After a soul-crushing hike, we made it as far as we could. The sun was setting, so we had to make camp before the animals came out and ate what little food we had left.

We got the tents up without any sword fights, which was a plus. A group of us stood around a circle of rocks we had created to encase our fire. Randy held a lighting stick to a bunch of kindling that was beneath a pile of damp fire wood. The flame danced in the breeze, but wouldn't take to the kindling.

"This stupid wood," Randy said.

Derek grabbed the lighter from Randy and said, "Here, let me do it."

Randy rolled his eyes and backed away.

Derek grabbed a few random leaves and placed them beneath the kindling. He clicked the lighter, the flame appearing from within. He held it to the leaves, which promptly curled and blackened, but didn't maintain the fire long enough to light the kindling.

"What can we burn?" Derek asked. He looked at me and said, "Give me your shirt."

"No," I scoffed. "First of all, it's wet. Second of all, use your shirt."

"We're all soaked," Sophie said. "There's not a dry thing around."

You know there's a problem when Derek Davenport can't light a fire. The kid leads the league in flaming bags of poo in our state. It's not official, but I would bet his bank account on it.

Derek tried again. He clicked the lighter, but it failed to ignite. He tried again. Nothing. Derek held the lighter up to his ear and shook it. "I think we're out of butane."

"Oh, great," Regan said.

Cheryl looked at Just Charles and asked, "Do you have a lighter in there?"

"No," he said, sheepishly.

Mr. Muscalini asked, "How about a flint and steel?"

"Negatory," Just Charles said.

Everyone groaned.

"My mother doesn't let me play with fire," Just Charles said, digging himself further into a hole.

A few people chuckled.

"What are we gonna do? Rub two sticks together?" Randy asked.

"We need more than that," I said.

Tensions were rising. Randy scoffed, "Oh, now you're the stick expert?"

"I'm the science genius. I know what causes and deters fire."

We needed more heat. I looked up through the trees, blocking the sun from my eyes. We still had a little bit of time before the sun went down.

"What does a fire need?" I asked myself.

"Idiot," Randy muttered.

"Heat. Oxygen. How can we generate more heat without a lighter?"

I looked at Charles, hoping to God that he would actually have what I needed. "Do you have binoculars in there?"

His face lit up. "Yeah, I do!" He rummaged through his pack and produced a set of binoculars.

I grabbed them, studied them for a moment, and then unscrewed the lens from the end of the binoculars.

"You have a book in there?" I asked.

"Yes," Just Charles said, tentatively. "C.T. Walsh's new release."

I pursed my lips. "As much as it pains me to say it- we have to burn it."

"It's rubbish, anyway," Randy said. "That guy is so overrated."

"But he's very handsome," Nick said.

Regan shrugged and said, "Meh."

Just Charles produced the book and held it out toward

me. I grabbed it, but he didn't let go. I tugged. He tugged back.

"It's signed by C.T., himself!" Just Charles said.

"Sorry, buddy. You know he would be okay with it," I said. A bunch of us had met the wacky author at Comic Con and helped save his writing career.

"Give him a corn dog and he'll be good with it," Ben said.

"With spicy mustard," Sophie added.

"What are you guys talking about?" Randy asked.

We all ignored him. Just Charles handed over the book. "Sorry, C.T." I said. I tore out a bunch of pages and handed them to Sophie, Ben, and Sammie. "Crumple these up and place them underneath the kindling. I handed the rest of the book to Luke. "Use the whole thing and the cover, too."

I looked back at the sun, contemplating the angle. I walked over to the edge of the campsite and searched the brush for branches.

"What are you looking for?" Derek asked.

"A branch shaped like a wishbone," I said, still searching.

Cheryl, Just Charles, Jayden, Dayna, and Mr. Muscalini joined the search.

After a few moments, Ditzy Dayna said, "I found one!" She held up a branch that split off into two branches like a wishbone.

"Yes!" I said, pumping my fist.

Dayna held it out, closed her eyes, and said, "I wish we had Wi-Fi." She then proceeded to snap the wishbone into two.

"Nooooo!" we all yelled.

"What?" Dayna asked. "That way, we could watch Netflix."

"You would think she would at least wish we got rescued," Ben muttered.

Mr. Muscalini said, "Keep looking. Never say die! Although, we might just die out here."

"I got one," Derek said.

Ditzy Dayna reached for it. "Let's make another wish!"

Derek hip checked her out of the way and handed it to me.

"Nobody touch this," I said. I dug the long, singular end into the ground beside the pile of wood, kindling, and fabulous literary prose, making sure the angle lined up with the sun.

I placed the binocular lens into the wishbone, which acted like a cradle. I pushed it down into the wishbone so it was nice and snug. The sun beam hit the lens with its full power.

"Now, we wait," I said.

After a few minutes, the literary genius of C.T. Walsh started to smoke. We watched with anticipation. After another minute, the award-winning prose burst into flames. We all cheered.

"Luke, you're full of hot air. Can you blow on this?" I asked.

"Very funny," he said, crouching down next to the fire.

Luke leaned toward the fire and started fueling it with air. The perfect pages raged with flames and spread to the small kindling.

"Yeah, baby!" Luke yelled.

"Let's say this ridiculous idea actually worked," Randy said, ignoring the fact that it had already worked. "What are we going to eat?"

Ben said, "I think Charles still has a few cans of beans."

"I do!" he said.

"But no can opener," Cheryl said, rolling her eyes.

"We have an axe," Randy said. "We'll just chop it in half."

I shook my head. I loved it when Randy was wrong. "Great. And then beans will fly everywhere."

"Have a better idea?" Randy asked, annoyed.

"I'll just karate chop it," Mr. Muscalini said, stepping forward. He closed his eyes and held his hands in prayer position, breathing deeply.

Sammie stepped forward and lowered Mr. Muscalini's hand for him. "That didn't turn out so well last time and that was wood. This is metal."

"Fair point, Ms. Howell," Mr. Muscalini said.

I said, "I have a better idea. Not everything can be done with brute force."

"You sure about that, Davenport?" Mr. Muscalini said, opening his eyes.

I said, "Let's use the axe-"

Randy chuckled, annoyed. "Yeah, great idea."

I continued, "if we use a little brains and brawn, I think we can get it done." I looked at Derek and said, "Dent both sides of the can with the butt of the axe."

Mr. Muscalini nudged Luke and said, "He said, butt." Both of them laughed.

Derek took the axe out of Randy's hand, placed one of the cans on the ground and smacked it with the back of the axe, leaving a nice indentation. He turned it over and smacked the other side.

"Now what?" Derek asked, holding up the can.

"Get a plate or a bowl. Mr. Muscalini can work the can back and forth until it breaks open."

Sammie said, "Nice idea."

"Thanks," I said.

Mr. Muscalini took the can and started wiggling it, while Derek dented the second can. We all watched him, while holding our breath. Our stomachs grumbled at the possibility of food. Ben held a bowl underneath the can. It seemed to take forever, but eventually, the can cracked open. Beans spilled onto the plate below.

We broke out into a raucous cheer. Ditzy Dayna kicked her leg up like she did on the football sidelines whenever Randy or my brother scored a touchdown for the glorious Gophers. I don't think beans have ever been celebrated that much in the history of beans. Granted, I never studied bean history. I made note to ask Dr. Dinkledorf if we ever made it home. Even Randy was moderately excited.

Ben dispersed the beans as evenly as possible. Nick grabbed his bowl and didn't even bother to use a spoon. He just put the bowl to his lips and chugged the beans like it was a soup. In all fairness, it was a better soup than I'd ever seen at Cherry Avenue's cafeteria.

Randy, of course, had an issue with Ben's bean fairness. "Mr. Muscalini- since we're all elite athletes over here," he said, pointing to himself, Nick, Jayden, and Derek. "Don't you think we should get more beans? Our muscles need more calories."

Mr. Muscalini weighed Randy's pitch.

"That's not fair. We're in survival mode. Not muscle-building mode," I said.

Mr. Muscalini pondered the question, perhaps wondering if there was ever not a time to build muscle. The non-athletes all put on our best starving faces. Our lives hung in the balance.

Mr. Muscalini looked down at his beans and started eating. "I'm too hungry to make a decision. Let's dig in."

I grabbed my beans and ate them as quickly as possible, before anyone could make a decision to take them away.

Mr. Muscalini said, "These are good, Zaino. I'm going way over on my carb intake, but still." And then he started to sing, "Beans, beans. Good for your heart, the more you eat, the more you fart!"

"What are you singing, coach?" Randy asked.

"You guys don't know the bean song? You need better adults in your life."

I nodded. "You couldn't be more correct, sir."

After a luxurious dinner of canned beans on top of canned beans, garnished with more beans (but not that many), we continued to set up our campsite.

Randy walked over to Just Charles. "Hey, Zaino. I need the rope that we used on the river."

"Okay," he said, somewhat afraid. "For what?"

"Since there's no food to tie up, I'm going to set a few snare traps, just in case the bears come looking for food and we're the only thing they find." He looked at me and smirked. Nice job again, Davenfart."

Just Charles found the rope and gave it too Randy. Randy tossed the long rope over the limb of a tree. I hoped he would get stuck in it himself and spend the night dangling upside down. Rumor had it that our custodian, Zorch, at Cherry Avenue Middle School used to catch kids in snare traps when they entered his lair.

While my standing in the tribe had certainly improved after starting the fire and opening the can of beans, the reminder of a lack of food and who was responsible for that definitely dampened everyone's enthusiasm for having me around. I needed to get everyone to forget about that. I was gonna have to beat Randy at his own game. He seemed to gain a lot of standing by chopping wood. I decided I would do the same.

I walked over to a long log that sat at the edge of the campsite, the axe sticking out of it. I grabbed it and pulled. It was stuck in there pretty good. I remembered that Nick had chopped a few pieces of wood from it. He was the strongest kid there. By far.

"Great," I muttered.

I put one foot on the log to hold it down and grabbed the axe handle with both hands. The damp wood cooled my hands. I tugged on the axe, but it didn't budge. I tried again, to no avail. I looked around to make sure no one had been watching my failures. Thankfully, nobody cared what I was doing. At least, it was good at that moment. I leaned in real close to the axe, wriggled it side to side, trying to loosen it. I pulled with both hands, pushed off the log with my leg, and let out a massive grunt, while trying not to fart. The axe slid from the log, the momentum carrying the axe and my arms up and behind my head. The wet handle slipped from my grip, the axe tomahawking through the air behind me.

I turned and yelled, "Look out!"

My eyes widened as the axe headed straight for Sophie. She looked up in horror, the axe descending toward her beautiful face. She screamed and jumped out of the way. Sophie landed with a thwack while the axe blade buried into the mud, only a few inches from her foot. She grabbed her ankle and writhed in pain.

I ran over to her and knelt next to her. "Are you okay?" I asked. "The axe was stuck and then slipped from my hand."

A crowd gathered around us.

Sophie sat up. "I think it's all right."

Ben, Luke, and I helped her to her feet.

"Owww," she yelped, as her left foot took on her weight.

"Looks like a sprain," Mr. Muscalini said. "Shouldn't be an issue."

"We have to walk a few miles tomorrow," Just Charles said.

Mr. Muscalini said, "That might be an issue."

Sophie hobbled around in a circle, testing her ankle.

"How does it feel?" Sammie asked, as we all looked on, concerned.

"Not great," she said, annoyed.

Everyone appeared to be staring at me, so I bent down to pick up the axe and avoid eye contact. Randy pulled the axe from my hand.

"Give me that, Davenfart. It's not a toy!" Randy said, shaking his head.

I walked over to Sophie. "I'm really sorry. It was an accident."

Sophie winced in pain. "You're just an accident waiting to happen," she said, annoyed.

I didn't know what to say. Tears welled up in my eyes, but I didn't want to cry in front of Randy. I wouldn't survive the ridicule, so I just walked away, defeated.

16

I sat on a rock alone, staring into the woods. My mind raced with thoughts I'd rather not share. Frustration seeped through my pores. Why was I such a klutz? Why did I always make things worse? I wondered if everyone would be better off if I just wandered away into the woods. I wondered how long it would take for them to even notice I was gone.

My pulse skyrocketed as I heard leaves rustle behind me. Randy had talked about me getting eaten by a bear so often, I was starting to believe it was a major possibility. I wondered if it might even be one of my better options out there. I stood up and got into my best kung fu stance, which wasn't all that good, especially when fighting bears, but my tiny fists of fury were all I had.

Thankfully, Mr. Muscalini emerged from the brush, a shovel in hand.

I took a deep breath and relaxed. "You coming to bury me?" I joked.

"No, I, ummm, just had to do some...gardening back here," he said, obviously not wanting to discuss what he had really just done. He looked at my face and raised an eyebrow. "What are you doing out here? You okay?"

"Not really. Nobody wants me around. I don't blame them," I said, sitting back down on the rock.

Mr. Muscalini sat down next to me. "You ever go rock climbing, Davenport?" He looked me up and down. "Who am I kidding? With those spindly legs, of course you haven't. My point is, besides the fact that you have obviously been skipping leg day your whole life, sometimes climbers have to make difficult decisions. Someone is dangling from the rope, useless, with the risk of pulling everyone down with him."

I wasn't sure where he was going with the conversation. Maybe he was there to bury me. I scooted back a foot, just in case.

Mr. Muscalini continued, "So, the climber above them has to cut the line and let them go to save everyone else."

"Umm, I'm not following you," I said. Was he trying to tell me he was going to cut me loose in the wild? Leave me for dead? My heart pounded.

"Make yourself useful. Dig a trench around the campsite to keep us from taking on water."

"Okay," I said, grabbing the small shovel from Mr. Muscalini's hulking hands. I looked up at him. "Is that it?"

"I think I've been pretty clear," he said, getting up.

"That's debatable," I muttered to myself.

I stood up and walked back to the edge of the campsite. I studied it for a minute, decided on the path for the trench, and plunged the mini shovel into the ground. It sliced a few inches into the wet earth with ease, but quickly met with thick resistance. I made another go of it, but was rejected again. I decided that was deep enough. I could only do what I could do.

I wasn't able to dig a deep trench, but I used the excess dirt to create a wall. It was the puniest wall I'd ever seen, but still, it was a wall. And it was going to protect us. It would stand the test of time, like the Great Wall of China. I really believed that until Mr. Muscalini hocked a loogie and nearly destroyed the whole thing. I shrugged and kept digging.

Eventually, I had squared off the entire campsite with a small trench. I was nearly done. I just had a few more feet to dig behind Randy's tent. I wondered if I should even do it. I wasn't sure he deserved my help. He certainly wouldn't appreciate it. But I did it anyway. Mainly out of fear, but still, I did it.

It had stopped raining, but huge drops were still falling from the trees. They fell on my head and back as I hunched over to shovel. I felt something on my neck. At first, I thought it was a drop of rain, but then I noticed it was moving up my neck and not down via gravity.

As you may remember from my battle with the giant spider in the utility closet at school during the science fair, I'm not big on bugs trying to eat me. My normally rational brain flipped the switch to panic. I reached behind my head and swiped at the bug. The precision of my karate attack was spot on, as usual. I looked down to see a spider scurrying away.

"Not so fast, punk!" I yelled.

I raised the shovel above my head and slammed it down on top of the spider. The shovel reverberated from the force of the massive blow. I lifted the shovel, satisfied that I had slain the beast, but I was mistaken. It had survived! Anger surged through my body. All of the frustration that had been building up during the trip were about to be taken out on that spider.

I wielded the shovel like a knight cutting down his

enemies on the battle field. Blow after blow, I pummeled the spider. There were cracks and thwacks echoing throughout the camp. Dirt flew. I may have even yelled, "Die, arachnid scum!"

I stopped beating the very dead spider, exhausted, but exhilarated by my glorious victory on the field of battle.

"Austin! What the heck are you doing?" Sophie asked.

Randy screamed, "Davenfart! You ruined my tent!"

I turned around, not sure what was going on. I was sure Randy was getting his panties in a bunch over nothing. My eyes widened as I saw Randy's tent half collapsed, two tent poles cut clean in half, the roof partially unsecured due to a sliced rope, and flopped open. What's worse was that the edge of the roof landed in the fire. Mr. Muscalini was stomping it out with massive blows.

"There was a...I was being attacked!" I said, defensively.

"You're gonna be attacked again," Randy said, stepping forward, his fists balled.

Mr. Muscalini stepped in front of Randy. "Take a step back, Warblemacher. It'll be fine."

I walked over to inspect the roof. "Yeah, it'll be fine," I said, echoing Mr. Muscalini.

The rain started to pick up again, which was kind of a problem when you were responsible for a roofless tent. "Let's just get this right back on," I said, grabbing an edge.

"Yeah, not an issue," Ben said, grabbing the other side.

We flipped the roof back across the top of the tent. I was able to take the sliced rope, which no longer stretched to the ground, and tie it to the tent, securing it tightly. Ben did the same.

I looked at our handy work. "See? Not an issue." I bit my lip as I looked at the roof's gaping hole, eaten by the fire.

"Well, it's your tent now, Davenfart! We're taking yours!" Randy said, nearly ripping the zipper off the door to his/my tent.

"That's cool. It's great for star gazing," I said.

Randy called from inside the tent, "The sky is filled with clouds and it's raining, you idiot."

The boys all grabbed their stuff out of the leaky tent and moved in to ours. Just as Randy was about to toss Just Charles' backpack out of the tent and into the mud, Mr. Muscalini said, "Nobody is sleeping in a tent without a roof. All the boys in one tent."

Ahhh, farts.

∾

THE REST of the night was on the quiet side. I was back to being public enemy number one, so I just kept to myself, not wanting to hurt anyone or break anything. I sulked at the edge of the campsite while everyone dried out around the fire.

I stood up and walked toward the tent without saying a word. I unzipped it, entered, and settled in for the night. I couldn't hurt anyone or mess anything up if I was asleep. Or so I thought.

Eventually, the fire went out and all the boys piled into the tent for the night. I pretended I was asleep so I wouldn't have to talk to anyone and hoped that meant nobody would ridicule me if they thought I couldn't hear it.

It was a tight squeeze. With the oversized Mr. Muscalini and Nick, coupled with the fact that we had three too many people in the tent than recommended by the manufacturer (who I made a note to contact and complain about the flimsiness of their ropes and non-fire retardant roof), which meant that there was a 50/50 chance that I would suffocate as we all jostled for air among too many limbs and sleeping bags.

Just as everyone had settled in for the night and said less-than-enthused good nights, a brain-rattling fart exploded on the far side of the tent.

"Gross!" Randy said, as nearly everyone in the tent, except for Mr. Muscalini, now resided on one side of the tent.

I groaned after Ben elbowed me in the ribs.

Mr. Muscalini said, "I make no apologies. It's natural. If I'm being honest, you should blame it on Zaino. He brought the beans."

"You would all be starving if I hadn't brought the beans!" Just Charles said, defensively.

"But not farting," Randy added.

Mr. Muscalini broke out into song. "Beans. Beans. Good

for the heart. The more you eat, the more you fart. The more you fart, the better you feel, so eat your beans...in...every... meal," he finished the song with a voice two octaves lower than normal.

Another fart rang out, perhaps burning a hole right through the bottom of the tent.

"Come on!" Randy yelled.

I didn't like the smell. I didn't like Ben sleeping on top of me. I didn't like sharing a tent with Randy and Nick. But I thoroughly enjoyed how much Randy hated it all.

Mr. Muscalini didn't seem to care. He sang out, "Everybody now! Beans. Beans...Hit the high notes, Davenport!"

"There are no high notes in the beans song," I mumbled.

"Oh, no?" he asked.

And then somebody, and I'm sure you can figure out who, let out a squeaker of a fart. It was so high pitched, I was worried that it might send a signal to any wolves or coyotes in the area. I wasn't sure if there were any, but we didn't need that kind of company.

"Gross," I heard Sophie say from the other tent.

"They're so disgusting," Sammie said.

"That wasn't me!" I called out.

Randy didn't agree. "Yeah, right. That's why everybody calls you, Davenfart."

"You're the only idiot who calls me that."

"Boys, enough," Mr. Muscalini said. "We're supposed to bond over flatulence, not fight."

I heard Ditzy Dayna ask the girls, "Are we gonna have a farting contest? Sounds like they're having fun over there."

"Umm, no," Sophie said, seemingly choking back her beans.

"That's my girl," Luke said, apparently stink struck with Dayna.

The farts continued to blast the tent. Everyone blamed me for burning the roof off the other tent, but I was pretty certain somebody was gonna blow our new roof right off. There were a lot of accusations and denials, along with a few attempts to restart the Beans song, but eventually everyone fell asleep. Except for me. Mr. Muscalini snored like a bear. Rain pelted the top of the tent, keeping me awake. Every so often, the storm would intensify and all the rain would seemingly meld together like a giant stream of pee on our tent. And it made *me* have to pee. I tried to hold it as long as I could as I lay snug in my sleeping bag, albeit squished, but eventually the urge to go was too strong.

The rain had died down a little, so I decided to make a go of it. I slipped out of my sleeping bag, into my sneakers, and then out of the tent. The fresh air was much needed. I left the door open a tad to keep the rest of the group from dying from the concentration of fart fumes. Of course, I got no thanks for that.

The ground outside was a muddy mess. Each step was a challenge, the mud sucking my feet in with a 'thwarp'. I had to pull up each leg with both hands. I took huge strides, given how difficult each step was. I wanted to take fewer of them, plus I didn't want to wake anyone up with the suction-cup pop that resulted each time the mud released my foot.

But I made a terrible mistake. I took a huge step, stretching as far as I could. The mud engulfed my foot like a vise grip, leaving me stuck in a semi-split with no ability to move either leg. I looked around, hoping there weren't any nocturnal creatures around to mock me. Thankfully, the coast was clear to embarrass myself. I tried to lift my back foot off the ground. It didn't budge. I pulled, but it was like I was encased in concrete. I took some solace knowing that Han Solo from Star Wars had once been encased in

Carbonite against his own will. True, he had a formidable villain in Darth Vader who had done the vile act, while I had only myself to blame, but still. I was down on myself enough. I couldn't take another blow to my ego.

I thought for a minute, not sure what to do. One thing was for certain, though. I knew without a shadow of a doubt that I did not want anyone to see me like this. The last thing I needed was for Randy to wake up in the morning to find my statuesque self cemented to the ground in a precarious position.

I contemplated whether or not I should just try to fall over and break out of the mold. But I risked the encasing of my entire body in the mud-crete, which would be much worse than my situation at that time.

And then I had an idea. I would untie my shoes, leave them behind, and use leaves and quick steps to get myself to the grass behind the tents. I initiated my plan, loosening my feet from the sneakers, and grabbing a few leaves from the ground around me. With all my might, I pulled my back foot forward. It released from the sneaker with ease. I stood on one leg with a handful of leaves and a very relieved groin. I placed out a few leaves in front of me and went for it. I left my second sneaker behind and hit every leaf like I was on some sort of video game. I made it to the grass and thrust my hands in victory.

But I had not won anything. I felt something tighten around my leg. My first thought was a Boa Constrictor. I nearly peed on it. Not sure that is the way to escape a snake, it was just my natural response. Before I could do anything, my leg was jerked out from underneath me and I found myself hanging upside down from a tree by my ankle. Randy's snare trap had ensnared me. I was a third angry, a third scared, and half embarrassed. I'm sure there was an owl watching somewhere. I also think that being upside down was messing with my math skills.

My hands scraped against the ground. I looked around in the darkness not sure what to do. I saw a broken piece of the shovel only a few inches from my fingers. I reached and grabbed it. I felt the jagged edge of the plastic, but it didn't seem sharp enough to cut through the rope. The string from the tent's roof was much thinner.

I was stuck and I still had to pee so badly. I wondered if I should try to do it. I spent a solid five minutes mentally listing the pros and cons of peeing while suspended upside down. I ultimately decided that the logistics involved were a bit too complicated, so I decided against it. I was wet enough and didn't want to become the first nerd in history to pee on my own head. Maybe I'm giving nerds too much credit. Perhaps I was the only one who hadn't.

I racked my brain for ideas, as I continued to dangle upside down by my ankle. I reached for the rope, grunted and groaned, but my abs were too weak to lift my upper body. I immediately regretted never drinking any of the protein shakes that Mr. Muscalini had suggested to me. And then I heard to soul-crushing sound of a tent unzipping.

"Aaaahhh, farts," I said.

Sophie's voice said, "What's going on out here?"

"I'm fine," I said, totally not fine.

"Where are you?"

I thought for a moment about what to say. "I'm just hanging out in a tree behind the tent."

"What?" Sophie asked, shining a flashlight in my direction. "I can't see anything...except a foot. Oh, God, Austin."

Sophie exited the tent, followed by the rest of the girls, except for Regan. At least they were all my friends. There was still a chance that the guys wouldn't see me like this.

"If you must see me, go around the back of the tent, but watch out for any more snare traps. Or lay down a leaf floor heading this way."

Sophie was half disappointed and half empathetic.

"We should get Mr. Muscalini," Sammie said.

"No-" I said, but was cut off by Ditzy Dayna.

"Mr. Muscalini! We need help!" Dayna yelled.

"Aaaahhh, farts. Again," I said, swinging in the breeze.

Within a few minutes, the entire camp surrounded me, gawking at my predicament.

It was difficult to tell because I was upside down and nearly all the blood in my body had pooled in my head, but I was pretty certain it was the funniest thing any of them had ever seen. It wasn't that difficult to figure out because Randy pointed at me, laughing hysterically, and said, "This is the funniest thing I've ever seen!"

"Shut up, Randy," Derek said, shaking his head, seemingly embarrassed. He was embarrassed of my existence when I was standing upright. I could only imagine how embarrassed he was with me upside down in a snare trap.

I was just thankful that nobody had a phone to take a picture of me in that state. It would've been a Derek Davenport special.

"If you're finished gawking, perhaps someone could help me down?" I asked, annoyed.

Mr. Muscalini said, "I warned you that we might have to cut the rope."

Randy laughed. "If only I had my cellphone. This would go viral."

"Sorry to disappoint you."

"It's okay, Davenfart. It will forever be burned in my mind. I can return to it whenever I need a good laugh."

Mr. Muscalini interrupted the conversation, "Okay, boys. Enough chit chat. Help him down."

Randy whined, "Aww, come on, coach. Just one more minute."

"Okay."

"What?" my crew and I yelled in unison.

Mr. Muscalini shook his head like it was his life's greatest disappointment. (It wasn't even mine.) He said, "Oh, alright. Get him down, pronto. Nice snare trap, by the way, Warblemacher. If only our football defense was as good. The Gophers would be unstoppable."

Just Charles handed Mr. Muscalini a pocket knife, which he used to whittle away at the rope above my ankle, none of us worried about what would happen when the one rope became two. By the time I realized it should be a concern, I landed on my head in the soft mud.

"Are you okay?" Sophie asked.

"Bloody terrific," I said, channeling my English heritage.

"Let's help you up," Mr. Muscalini said.

"Just leave me here," I said. "Save yourselves." I couldn't bare to look at Sophie. It was dark, but my face was bright red or maybe I just landed face first in the fire.

17

We were back in the tent packed like sardines, but smelling far worse, which I didn't realize was possible. I was soaked to my core, but the warmth of the sleeping bag did help. But there was so much tossing and turning that with my eyes closed, I thought I was at a bad DJ record-spinning contest. It was not exactly conducive to sleeping. Not to mention, it was raining again with both thunder and lighting, which randomly shook the ground and lit up our tent.

"I can't sleep," Jayden said.

Randy said angrily, "You can thank Davenfart for that."

"Yeah, he controls the weather," Ben said, defending me.

"Do you ever shut your mouth?" I asked Randy.

"I'll say what I want when I want to. And I'd be careful if I were you...Oh, God. I'd hate to be you," Randy said.

"The feeling is mutual," I spat.

Lighting struck again. Somehow, Mr. Muscalini was snoring.

"What the-" Derek said.

"Did you pee?" Jayden asked, annoyed.

Derek scoffed. "No, did you?"

"I feel wet," Nick said.

"Nick peed himself!" Luke said, obviously without thinking.

"Watch it, Davenfart!" Nick yelled.

Fear surged through my body. "It wasn't me!" I yelled.

"Oh, God. We're taking on water!" Randy yelled.

Mr. Muscalini woke up. "What's all the fuss about? Why is my pillow wet?"

"We're taking on water," Randy said, annoyed.

Everyone sat up. Flashlights popped on. It was very clear that water had made its way through the wall of the tent.

Mr. Muscalini looked at me. "Did you dig the trench?"

"Yes," I said, as confidently as I could, remembering how Mr. Muscalini's wad of spit had knocked down my wall.

"How deep?" Mr. Muscalini asked.

"I don't know," I shrugged.

Everyone groaned, as we all shuffled to the door side of the tent, making it even cozier.

Mr. Muscalini said, "Warblemacher and Davenport- get out there and dig the trench deeper."

Randy scoffed, "What about you, sir?"

"I'm too cozy. I mean, you two need to man up. And my hand is broken!"

"Unbelievable," Randy muttered.

My thoughts exactly. I was already wet, so the rain wasn't the problem, although I'm not a big fan of lightning, despite my love of science. It was that I had to spend time with Randy and his seemingly endless supply of rudeness.

I slipped on my sneakers and headed back out to see what to make of the trench. Randy and I walked around to the back where the water had breached the tent. I looked down at the wall, or where I thought the wall was supposed to be. It was nonexistent. Water had filled the trench and the rain had washed it away. The loogie should've made me realize that.

"Nice work, Davenfart. You can't dig a trench, but you seem to keep digging us deeper and deeper into a giant mess."

Lightning cracked and lit up the sky.

"What am I supposed to do out here?" Randy asked, annoyed.

"You can start by shutting your mouth," I spat. "Is it even capable of doing that?"

Lightning cracked again. "Just hurry up, Davenfart. I don't want your slow butt getting mine killed."

I stopped digging and said, "Well, if you're such a trench-digging expert, maybe you should've dug it!"

I pushed the cracked shovel into Randy's chest a lot harder than I wanted to.

Randy tossed the shovel aside, lowered his shoulder, and flattened me like a pancake. I splattered into the mud on my back, as I struggled to get away from the Randy Psychomacher.

"The Camel Clutch is coming for ya, Davenfart!" The Camel Clutch was the deadliest of all wrestling moves and I had succumbed to it more often that any middle schooler I knew, not to mention also leading the league in getting duct taped to the wall in school. If Cheryl hadn't been on the school newspaper, I'm sure they would keep stats on it in the Gopher Gazette.

Lightning struck again. Wood chips exploded in every direction as the bolt blasted a tree on the outskirts of the woods. I looked up, Randy straddling my back, nearing the Camel Clutch lock under my chin. My eyes widened as the tree split midway up, slowly peeled off the main trunk like a

Band Aid, and then toppled over. I yelled out, "Gurrgle flimmer tree frwalling!"

Randy didn't move even though I thought I had been very clear. What was certainly clear to me was that I was going to die in the Camel Clutch, my particles enmeshed with Randy's for all eternity, as we were surely about to die.

18

Fearing that Randy's dark heart would overpower my angelic self, leading to our enmeshed selves getting sucked down to Hell for all eternity, I took matters into my own hands. Actually, my elbow. As hard as I could, I thrust my elbow behind me blindly. It connected with Randy's face. His grip underneath my chin loosened. I rolled to the side, taking him with me, and yelled, "Ahhhh, farts!" I ended up on my back, looking up as the tree crashed down beside us with a thud and a splatter of mud and tree bark.

Screams echoed from the rest of the crew. Randy lay to my left and the tree to my right. We were both huffing and puffing, partially from the struggle, but also in a near panic because we almost died. The flashlight illuminated us. I looked over at Randy, both our eyes wide. We sat up without saying anything.

The crew rushed out to see what had happened.

"Are you okay?" Sophie shrieked.

Still partially in shock, I said, "I think so." I looked around, surveying the scene. The only casualties were the tree, obviously, and the shovel, which had been shattered to bits.

Randy apparently shook off the shock more quickly than I did. He said, "Look what you did now, Davenfart! The shovel is broken."

"I just saved your life and you care about the shovel?" I yelled, in even more shock than I already was in.

Regan rushed to Randy and dove onto him. "Oh, my baby! Are you okay, Randy Wandy?"

"I'm fine," he said, annoyed.

Mr. Muscalini helped me up. Sophie wrapped her arms around me.

Randy bumped my shoulder as he walked by. "Just stay away from me."

"I always do. You're the one who's always on my case," I said.

I continued hugging Sophie, but then she backed away. I whispered, "Are we friends again?"

"I'm glad you're okay," she said, monotone, not answering my question.

I let go and walked away without saying anything. I was tired of everyone being mad at me for stuff that wasn't my fault.

"Okay, everyone. Back to bed," Mr. Muscalini said.

We followed orders and slipped back into our tents. As we lay in our sleeping bags, I tried to push the day's terrible events out of my mind.

"What the heck happened?" Ben asked.

"The universe hates me," I said, simply.

"Seems like just the opposite. You could've been toast."

"If only," I said, rolling over and turning my back on Ben.

〜

I woke up early again the next morning. I sat on the lightning-struck tree, staring off into the woods.

Ben sat down next to me. "You okay?" he asked.

"Not really. And how are you on this fine morning?" I asked, sarcastically.

"A little better than you. I didn't almost kill my girlfriend."

I scoffed, "I had nothing to do with the tree! Now I control the weather? If only. I wouldn't be soaked down to my underwear."

"Thanks for that tidbit of info, but I was talking about the axe-throwing incident," Ben said.

"Oh, that," I said. So much had happened since then, I nearly forgot. "There's still today, but I'm going to try my hardest to avoid that."

Ben said, "She's still really mad at you. I talked to her this morning."

"She'll get over it," I said. "It's not the first time I almost killed her."

"True, but you did almost kill her and that's not something easily shrugged off."

I shrugged. "It was an accident. Our love will never die. It's like a blossoming flower."

Ben said, "Flowers die all the time."

Mr. Muscalini emerged from the brush in front of us, looked down at a small flower, and stomped on it.

"See?" Ben said.

"Well, this has been really uplifting, but I gotta poo. You have any toilet paper?"

"Wipe your butt with a leaf," Ben said.

"Really? There's poison ivy out there! Don't you have any?"

" I need it for me."

"Come on, dude," I said. "This is a friendship breaker."

"Okay, I'll give you a few squares."

"Thanks so much," I said, sarcastically.

I stood up and followed Ben to the tent. I took a deep breath when I saw Sophie. She limped across the campsite, her face attempting to hold in the pain, but not doing a very good job of it. She winced nearly every time her foot hit the ground.

I walked over to her. "Can I help you?"

"Haven't you *helped* enough?" Sophie asked, bitterly.

"That's fair. I deserved that. I think I can help you, though," I said, before I actually figured out how I could actually help her.

"How?" she asked, skeptically.

We didn't have ice, but I could perhaps stabilize her ankle, reducing the strain. I rushed over to the edge of the woods, grabbed a few sticks, tore out some vines that I hoped wasn't poisonous, and hurried back to Sophie.

"Sit down," I said.

She did as she was told. It was a first, I think. I tied a vine to one of the sticks. The vine promptly broke. I tried again. Same result.

"Hey, Charles. I need some string," I said.

"The stuff I have is much thicker than that vine," he said. "But I have just the thing." Just Charles grabbed his pack and rifled through it. He pulled out a tiny mandolin.

"What the heck?" Sophie said.

I scratched my head. "Why did you bring that? Do you even play...whatever that is?" I asked.

"It's a mandolin," Just Charles said. "No, I don't play it, but I thought somebody might like to use it around the campfire."

"Ummm, great thinking," I said. "Can you de-string it?" I asked, not sure if that was even a word.

Just Charles said, "I think so."

Within a few minutes, I was wrapping mandolin strings around Sophie's foot, securing them to the sticks I used to immobilize her ankle from bending side to side.

"Is that tight enough?" I asked.

"I think so," Sophie said, trying to wiggle her ankle.

"Good as new," I said, cheerfully. I instantly knew I shouldn't have said it.

Sophie smirked. "Yeah, right."

"You're really mad at me?" I asked. "Did you expect me to be Paul Bunyan out here?"

"No, but I didn't expect you to almost kill me, either," Sophie said, and then hobbled away, leaving me with a mandolin with no strings. I couldn't even play a sad song. It was pathetic.

19

Mr. Muscalini stood in the middle of the campsite. "Let's go. Gottá break down camp and hit the trails and where's that shovel? I gotta, well, dig a hole."

Ben said, "It's broken, sir. The tree, remember?"

"Oooh, that's going to be a bit of a problem," he said. "Well, after I come back, nobody walk back there. That mud might not actually be mud."

"I'm so hungry," Randy said. "Why don't we have any food? Oh, I remember, Davenfart forgot to protect it from the animals."

"You're still complaining about that?" I asked.

Randy said, "Uhhh, yeah. What do you want me to say? It's okay, Davenfart. I know you didn't mean to starve us." He rolled his eyes and walked away.

I tried to be helpful in cleaning up the camp site. But wherever I went, it appeared to be the place that nobody else wanted to be. I went to help Sammie fold her sleeping bag.

"I'm good," she said, not looking up a me.

I walked over to Luke. "Let me get that pack for you," I said, smiling.

"I got it, man," he said. He threw the pack on his shoulder and walked away.

I walked over to Derek and Jayden, sitting on the dead tree. "You guys want to help me take down the tent?"

"We're a little busy," Derek said, while doing absolutely nothing. "But you go right ahead."

I shook my head. "Thanks," I muttered.

If nobody wanted to be around me, I decided I would just do everything myself. I walked over to our tent. I undid the stakes around the edges. I figured that would be an easy task, given that they were only a few inches deep into the mud.

While I was busy working, the girls were busy complaining.

"My nails look terrible," Sammie said.

"Have you seen my hair?" Sophie asked.

Sammie laughed, "More than you," she said, widening her eyes.

Sophie chuckled.

"Is my mascara running?" Ditzy Dayna asked. Yes, the girls still attempted to wear makeup in the wilderness.

I looked over at Dayna. She had more mascara on her cheeks than on her eyelashes.

Mr. Muscalini stepped forward. "Some of us have broken hands. Others, broken spirits," he said, looking at me. "Yet others need to shave their heads." Sophie frowned, patting her hair. "Don't think of yourselves as middle school girls. Think of yourselves as tribal warriors! There was a tribe in South America that was led by powerful women."

"Oh, that sound about right," Cheryl said.

Mr. Muscalini continued, "They also ate the weak for dinner."

"Not as right," Cheryl said.

"Only the strong survive. It's a wonder Davenport hasn't been eaten already," Mr. Muscalini said.

"Great. Thank you for your support, sir."

"Always happy to help."

Just Charles walked over to me with the map. "You should lead the way."

"Do you think anybody here wants me leading the way? Or even be here, for that matter?"

Randy walked over before Just Charles could answer. "Give me that, nerds," Randy said, with a snarl. "You've done enough."

I shook my head. "I'm gonna go for a walk," I said to Just Charles.

"Don't get eaten!" Mr. Muscalini said.

"Or do," Randy said. "I want to buy my girl something pretty with my winnings."

Regan melted. "Aww, you're so sweet."

Nobody said anything. Nobody cared that I was leaving.

20

I wandered through the woods, careful to remember important landmarks so I could make my way back. I just walked and walked, no destination in mind. I think I just wanted to get as far away from the campsite as possible, a terrible reminder of the situation we were in.

I walked through a wooded trail that opened up into a grassy area in front of a pond. I walked down to the water, not sure if the fish had two heads or not. I wished I had turned back earlier. I turned around and nearly jumped out of my shoes. A man with long, black hair and a bushy beard stood in the path I had just walked from. The sun reflected off his machete.

"Hey, there," he said. "You lost or somethin'?" The man picked his teeth with the machete. "You ever get bear meat stuck in your teeth?" he asked.

"I'm not lost. My group is only a few minutes behind," I said, nervously. I stared at the machete.

"Is this making you nervous?" the man asked.

"A little bit," I lied. I wished I had a diaper.

The man tossed the machete at me. It soared through the air, slicing into the ground only about a foot in front of my toe.

"Here, take that. If it makes you feel safe."

"Ok. It does. I have killed a bear with my bare hands, but you take that."

I looked at the machete and then the man. "You are so welcoming. It's a wonder you haven't turned this fine place into a bed and breakfast," he said.

The man chuckled. He walked toward me. I picked up the machete. I wasn't sure how to use it, but it couldn't be too hard.

"Are you gonna eat me?" I asked, nervously.

You ain't got no meat on ya, boy," he said. "I'm just kidding. I don't need meat. I'll just use your bones for a necklace."

"What?" I asked, desperately trying not to pee down my leg.

"I'm just kidding. Have a seat," he said and then plopped down at my feet, staring out into the pond.

I wasn't sure if I should just run or stick around and get the guy to help us. He did hand over his machete, so I figured he could've killed me, but didn't.

"Do you have a phone or some way to message for help?" I asked, and then clarified, "Not from you. At least I don't think. We got separated from our group."

"Are there any adults with you?" the man asked.

"Yes. One very large gym teacher. We've got an axe and a shovel that can slice through tent poles," I said, trying to deter him from taking me out.

"I don't communicate with the outside world. I came here to get away from all that," he said. "My name's Ron. What's yours?"

Ron didn't seem like a scary name. "Austin," I said. "You don't miss interacting with people?"

He shrugged. "Not really. I am at peace out here. I talk to the squirrels."

"Do they talk back?"

"No," he said, laughing. "Sometimes I put on a Big Foot costume and scare the campers and hikers."

"How often do people come through?" I asked.

"Besides winter, most weekends. But with the storm like this, you're not gonna find anyone stupid enough to come out here. Well, besides you."

"Thanks. My self esteem is so strong right now, I can handle it."

"You're a feisty one, aren't ya?" Ron said. "What's on your mind?'

"Life." Perhaps the end of mine.

"Deep thoughts for a young kid," Ron said. We stared out at the lake. Ron said, "Life's like a river. You can't control it. So you gotta let it flow."

I asked, "Well, you can dam it up, can't you?"

"You can withdraw from life, but eventually the consequences will blow up on ya. Eventually, a dam bursts, too."

I didn't really understand what we were talking about. It was like a normal conversation with Mr. Muscalini.

Ron continued, "Control what you can control. Let the rest go. And don't pee up hill or into the wind. Those are very important life lessons that are best to learn from someone else than from experience."

"Good to know," I said. I raised an eyebrow. "Did you really kill a bear?"

"I did," Ron said.

"How did you do it without being scared?"

Ron smiled. "I didn't. I was scarder than I'd ever been." I wasn't sure scarder was a word, but I understood his point. "You gotta act despite the fear."

I shook my head. "I don't think I'm made to do that. Pee in my pants, maybe."

"I'm sure there have been times when you stood up in spite of your fear."

I thought for a minute. "I did punch a giant spider in the face once."

"That's somethin'," he said, unconvinced.

"It was a big spider," I defended. "I also battled my nemesis to the death in a sword fight," I added, excitedly.

"You killed him?" he asked, shocked.

"Well, no, but somebody could've died. Maybe. Probably not. But it was a big deal to me. I was outmatched, but I worked my butt off, and I gave him my best, even though he was bigger, stronger, and faster than me."

"Well, sounds like you got a foundation to build on."

"Since we're kind of friends now, can you help us? We need to contact the police, maybe a S.W.A.T. team. We're running low on food. Simple misunderstanding, really."

"The only communication you'll be able to do out here is face to face. I don't speak to nobody. Keep walking along the river, heading south and eventually you'll come to an inlet with a foot bridge."

"I didn't see the bridge on the map," I said, frowning.

"It's not. That'll take you to the closest town. There are camp grounds there. Some rafting adventure place."

"Thank you. I appreciate your help. And for not killing me with your bare hands."

Ron laughed. "Happy to help. Don't underestimate the power of decision. All you gotta do is decide who you want to be and the rest follows. I made a decision to come out here and I left all my problems behind. Haven't looked back."

"Yeah, but my situation is the opposite. I have to go back to my problems."

Ron laughed again. "True. That's a bit more difficult, but I think it works just the same. Decide what you want, who you want to be, and do it."

"What if I'm not good enough?" I asked.

"You do the best you can do. Make no apologies for that," he said. "Good luck," he said, standing up.

"Here, take this," I said, handing him the machete.

He smiled and exited the way we came.

I sat by that pond for a while. I lost track of time. I had to man up, but I didn't know how. But I made a decision that I would and that was enough to get started.

21

I returned to the campsite with a plan. I knew where we were going and I decided I was going to lead them there.

Ben ran up to me, followed by Sophie, and Just Charles. "You okay?" He asked.

"Never better," I said.

Sophie said, "We were worried about you."

Just Charles said, "We thought...well, we thought that Randy was gonna win his bet and get rich."

"That would've been terrible," I said.

Ben laughed. "Yeah, he would've been more *unbearable* than ever."

"And I would've been dead!"

Ben nodded. "Oh, yeah. There's that, too."

Sophie looked at me and raised an eyebrow. "You look different."

I said confidently, "I am different. I'm a man."

Ben questioned, "You had your bar mitzvah in the woods by yourself?"

"No. I'm not even Jewish. But I decided to man up. I don't

know how we're going to get out of this mess, but we're going to find a way. I just hope nothing else bad happens."

And just as I said those words, it all began to unravel. As if it was all nicely put together in the first place.

Mr. Muscalini walked into the campsite, chowing down on a handful of berries. Red berry juice encircled his lips like he was a kid who just drank too much fruit punch. "I'm so hungry," he said. "I don't usually eat a lot of fruit, but I am due for a carb reload day." He looked at Ben. "Hey Gordo, take some of these. They're good for your brain. Lord knows your brain could use 'em." The guy was unreal. He bashed our bodies all day, every day. Now our minds weren't even safe.

Ben shrugged and ate the berries. I didn't know everything about berry bushes, but I knew there were a bunch you didn't want to eat.

"Mr. Muscalini, I would be careful about eating too many of those. They could be dangerous," I said.

"Nonsense! I got a lot of muscle to fuel. I need the calories." Mr. Muscalini popped a few more berries into his mouth.

Just Charles said, "I've got a book in my pack about plants and stuff. I'll go get it."

Randy chimed in, "You don't need to look it up. The fruit he ate was the poison berry of the plantus posocantus."

Sophie rolled her eyes. "That's not real."

Mr. Muscalini put his finger on his berried chin. "You know what would go great with these? Honey!" Mr. Muscalini walked away from us, heading into the woods.

"Where is he going?" Cheryl asked. "Where are you going?" she called after him.

"A bee hive I found in the woods. There's probably honey in there. I'm sure it will go lovely with these berries."

"You can't just take out a handful of honey from a hive!" I yelled, running after Mr. Muscalini.

The rest of the crew followed me, as we surged into the woods, following a trail of swaying bushes and a rumbling stomach.

We came to a clearing and found Mr. Muscalini staring up at a bee hive. Before we could do or say anything, he put his hand in the hive.

Cheryl and Sophie yelled too late, "No!"

I closed my eyes, not wanting to see what would happen next. I waited. I didn't hear any buzzing, screaming, or shrieking. I slowly opened one eye and then the other. I thought he would be attacked by bees or maybe turn around to find himself competing with a bear for the honey, but nothing happened.

I took a deep breath, grateful that we avoided a disaster, not realizing that the disaster had already occurred. It was just in the process of metabolizing.

Just Charles said to Luke, "Do you know bees have a honey stomach and a regular stomach?"

"Really?" Luke asked. "I guess it makes sense. I have a regular stomach and a dessert stomach."

"There's no such thing," Just Charles laughed.

Luke said, "There definitely is."

Mr. Muscalini interrupted the riveting conversation by saying, "That was disappointing." He grabbed his throat softly and frowned. "I'm thirsty." He took the canteen from his waist and quickly chugged it. Without warning, he grabbed Randy's and chugged his, too. Before we knew what was going on, he downed Nick's water as well.

"Where's Ben?" I asked.

I turned around and found Ben, water dripping down his chin, and his empty canteen on its way to the ground. He grabbed Sammie's, popped the top, and started chugging.

"What the heck is happening?" Regan asked.

"The berries!" Sophie and I yelled, in unison.

"Don't let them drink your water!" I yelled.

But it was too late. Mr. Muscalini and Ben had devoured our water supply, seemingly a side effect of eating the poisonous berries that were most definitely not named whatever Randy thought they were named.

"We need to get moving," Just Charles said.

Sammie countered, "We can't leave without more water. It's a long hike."

"I found a short cut, so it won't be as long as we thought, but she's right," I said, agreeing with Sammie.

"Where are we gonna get more water?" Cheryl asked.

"I'm not drinking anyone's pee," Luke said.

"Nobody's drinking anyone's pee," I said.

Mr. Muscalini said, "Speak for yourself, Davenport. I'm so thirsty."

After we all threw up in our mouths, we decided we needed to find more water and quickly, before anyone did anything drastically disgusting.

"Where are we gonna get the water?" Derek asked.

"There's the river," I said. "And the puddles from the trenches."

"I'm not drinking Rotten River water," Randy said.

"For once, I agree with him," I said. I thought for a moment. "To the trenches!"

WE HURRIED over to the trench. It wasn't deep, but it encircled the camp, so there was a fair amount of water in it. The only problem was that it was muddy water. I grabbed an empty jug and scooped up a bunch of water from the trench. Dirt swirled around the jug.

"I'm not drinking that, either," Randy said.

"Why not just boil it?" Sophie said.

"Would you drink *that* boiled?" Regan responded.

I kind of agreed with her. "We have to filter it," I said.

"It looks like the water they must use to make the radioactive beef stew in the cafeteria," Luke said.

Ditzy Dayna said, "Oh, I love the radioactive beef stew. It has such a great flavor kick."

"Yeah, it's plutonium," Just Charles whispered.

" Okay. Let me think," I said. "We need to start a fire.

First step is to boil the water. I also need two empty water jugs and toilet paper."

"Dude, we don't need to know that you haven't wiped your butt," Randy said, disgusted.

"We're making a filter, you idiot," I said.

"Oh," Randy said, sheepishly.

"I also need some rocks, gravel, sand, and...some charcoal from the fire."

Luke asked, "Where are we going to get sand from? We're not near a beach."

"Can we go to the beach?" Dayna asked, excitedly.

"It doesn't have to be beach sand. Just find me different sizes of rocks and gravel. There should be some fine rock particles by the stream. The closest size to beach sand you can find, the better."

Everyone got busy collecting my list of ingredients.

I looked at Derek. "Can you chop the bottom off two of the water jugs?"

Derek looked around. "Yeah, I think so. I should be able to hack it off with the axe."

"Watch out. It might be slippery," Sophie said.

I threw her a smirk. It was better than a slippery axe.

Derek grabbed a water jug and the axe. He lined up the blade. It cut into the jug with ease. He worked the axe around the circumference of the jug until the bottom fell onto the ground. He then did the same to the second jug.

"Nice work," I said.

Just Charles, Cheryl, Luke, and Dayna returned with jugs of gravel and smaller rocks, almost as small as beach sand.

"This should be good, right?" Just Charles asked.

I looked at it and said, "Yep. Perfect."

Randy came over with toilet paper. "I still think you didn't wipe your butt," he said.

"Thanks," I said, ignoring his comment.

I took the toilet paper and layered it into the sliced-open jug, covering the spout. I used nearly the whole roll, creating a filter. I then took the second jug and slipped it inside, leaving enough room for water to pool up on top of the filter. I placed the larger rocks at the bottom of the second jug, then layered in smaller rocks, gravel, the sand, and charcoal on top.

"Hey, Nick?" I said.

"Yeah?"

I asked extra nicely, "Do you mind holding this jug while we pour the water into it?"

"Yep."

I wasn't sure if he minded or was actually going to help, but he walked over and grabbed the jug from me.

"Thanks," I said.

Derek walked over with a jug filled with dirty water.

I placed an empty jug on the ground beneath the one that Nick was holding. He squatted down and lined the spouts up.

Derek slowly poured the dirty water into the filter. The water trickled down through the different layers, dripped into the bottom jug with the toilet paper filter, and then into the empty jug underneath the filter. It slowly started to fill up, the water particle free.

"Yeah, baby!" I said.

Just Charles wound up for a high five. I aimed for his hand with gusto, but slipped in the mud, and kicked the filter. Nick steadied it with a glare that nearly caused my heart to explode.

I stood up and looked at Sophie. She looked at me, shook her head, and let a small smile break out.

I ignored the stares and said, "Now, we boil that."

"Wow, that's pretty cool," Regan said.

Randy shot a look at her. I tried to hide my smile, but I don't think I did a very good job of it.

"If we filter it, why do we still need to boil it?" Sammie asked.

"Because it could still have pathogens," I said.

Sophie nodded and said, "That was pretty awesome."

I looked at her with my hands on my hips and a raised eyebrow and asked, "Pretty awesome?"

Sophie smiled. "Just plain awesome."

"There was nothing plain about that," I said, faking annoyance.

Sophie shook her head, smiling.

In all of this, we forgot about Mr. Muscalini and Ben, but then we heard Mr. Muscalini scream.

He stared at Ben, his eyes wide and his face white. "Ahhh! Gordo! Why do you have two heads?" Without getting an answer from Ben, who was seemingly about to make out with a caterpillar climbing a tree, Mr. Muscalini yelled, "Dive roll!" He soared through the air like a swan, tucked, and rolled onto the ground. "That was fun!"

"They're delirious!" Luke said.

"You're just figuring that out now?" Just Charles asked.

Mr. Muscalini was on his knees, peering over the lightning-struck tree.

"What's he doing?" Cheryl asked.

I shrugged. "Probably talking to an imaginary rabbit or something."

Mr. Muscalini cooed, "Oh, pretty snake. So pretty. Give Mr. Mus a big kiss?"

"What? No!" I yelled, rushing over to Mr. Muscalini. Cheryl, Nick, and Derek all arrived at the same time.

We looked on in horror as a snake struck like lightning and bit Mr. Muscalini's cheek. Mr. Muscalini toppled over onto his back. He looked up into the sky and said, "Pretty rainbow..." And then he was silent.

Sophie, Sammie, and Cheryl all started to cry. Even Regan looked mildly concerned.

"Is he dead?" Regan asked. "He looks totally dead."

I felt like I was gonna puke.

22

B efore we could check on Mr. Muscalini, I saw the snake's head pop up above the dead tree, perhaps hungry for more. It slithered over the tree, as everyone scattered, leaving Mr. Muscalini unprotected on the ground, which I guess was okay if he was dead, but we didn't know for sure.

Emboldened by my rocket launcher of an arm that nearly destroyed a whole bridge, I picked up a rock, closed my eyes, and threw it as hard as I could. The rock, or perhaps I should call it a rocket, soared over Mr. Muscalini, missed the snake by a millimeter, or possibly a meter (Can we pretend I'm just not good at math instead of a terrible rock thrower?), and then bounced off Mr. Muscalini's crotch.

Our entire crew groaned, even the girls.

"Derek, do something," I said.

Derek looked around, picked up a rock and hurled it at the snake. It connected with the snake's head and bounced off the tree with a crack. The slithering snake had lost its slither. And most of its head.

"Decent throw, Davenport," Randy said, coolly.

I rushed to Mr. Muscalini's side and put my hand on his chest. "He's still breathing."

Without warning, Mr. Muscalini's eyes exploded open. He grabbed my hand and said, "Pardon me, but do you have any Grey Poupon? I'd like to eat that snake with some tasty dijon mustard." With that, he passed out again.

"What the heck is happening?" Sammie asked, her voice rising an octave with each word.

Ben wandered over and looked at Mr. Muscalini. "The bear is hibernating. I always wanted to wrestle a bear. Flying elbow!" Ben yelled and dropped an elbow on Mr. Muscalini across his chest.

Mr. Muscalini opened his eyes again like nothing happened. "What a great nap," he said, lifting his face from the mud. "But my face hurts. It feels like the time I got kicked in the face by Kick! the Donkey."

"The donkey that chugs the energy drinks for that beverage company?" Nick asked.

"Yep," Mr. Muscalini said.

Luke said, "That's so cool!"

I wasn't sure what was cool about getting kicked by a donkey, but whatever. We had bigger issues. Ben was looking up Mr. Muscalini's nose, admiring his nose hair.

Ben said, "It's incredible up there!"

Everybody appeared to be safe for the moment, so I huddled up with Sophie, Derek, Jayden, Cheryl, and Just Charles.

"What do we do now?" Sophie asked, concerned.

Sammie and Cheryl were fighting back tears.

Jayden asked, "Should we eat it?"

"Eat what?" I asked.

"The snake. We're all starving," Jayden said.

"Are you crazy? It's poisonous," Just Charles answered.

"Is that bad? I'm hungry," Derek added.

I said, "Yes, it's bad. I think. I mean, it's gotta be."

"I'm sensing you're starting to come around on this," Derek said. He looked at Jayden, "Do you want snake on a stick?"

"Guys, we can't wait around to start cooking headless snakes, as appetizing as that sounds. We gotta get these two to a doctor."

Just Charles looked at his watch. "We've got eight hours before nightfall to make it to the rest of the group."

Luke joined in. "We should get the venom out. That's what they do in the movies."

Cheryl asked, "How do they do that?"

"Well, you'll have to suck on his face," Luke said, simply.

Cheryl shrieked, "What? Why me?"

I shook my head. "It's too late for that. It's already in his bloodstream."

"Yeah, we've gotta move and fast," Sophie said.

"How are we gonna carry Mr. Muscalini through the woods for miles?" Just Charles asked. "We can't even get ourselves through the woods quickly."

"Maybe don't pack a mandolin," Derek said, shaking his head.

"It was useful!" Just Charles said, defensively.

"We're done for," Luke said. "There's no way we can get Mr. Muscalini to safety."

"So, what? We should just give up and sit around starving?" I asked, frustrated.

"Well, there's the snake," Derek said.

"We're not eating the snake!" I yelled.

Regan said, "We can't do this."

Sophie and Cheryl had tears in their eyes. I felt my allergies acting up as well.

"I hate to say it, but we should just leave him here," Randy said.

"What? No!" I yelled.

"We're leaving," Randy said, nodding to Regan.

"So are we," I said. "With Mr. Muscalini."

"I'm not going with you," Randy spat.

"Austin should lead us," Just Charles said. "And you'd be stupid to separate from the rest of us."

Randy scoffed. "I don't need Austin Davenfart to lead me home."

Derek stepped forward. "Randy, shut your mouth. You're just jealous that he's a better leader than you."

Randy didn't shut his mouth. He scoffed. "He can't lead. You've seen him out here, getting knocked out, almost chopping off Sophie's foot, hanging from bear traps."

Sophie's voice shook as she said, "Speaking of bear traps. We could probably use one right about now."

I looked over to see a ginormous black bear on its hind legs, staring down at Sophie. She froze. Had I not been dehydrated, I probably would've peed. The bear roared, it's fabulous breath nearly causing my lungs to shut down. Sophie fell back to the ground.

Randy turned on his heels and sprinted away, leaving Regan and the rest of us in the dust, disappearing into the woods.

I froze, not sure what to do, but then I remembered Ron and how he acted in spite of his fear. I also remembered that you're supposed to act crazy in front of bears to scare them.

"Act crazy! We need it to be afraid of us!"

Just Charles added shakily, "Bears can't see well. Get in a big group!"

We all crowded around behind Sophie and started jumping around, waving our arms, and screaming. Just Charles rapped. Derek shadow boxed. Our three cheerleaders, Regan, Sammie, and Ditzy Dayna did a Cherry Avenue Gophers' cheer. "Go! Go! Go, Gophers!" Nobody said it was a good cheer. I'll never speak of it again, but I think Nick might've done the funky chicken dance.

The bear dropped to all fours, turned, and ran into the woods in the opposite direction of Randy.

"Huzzah!" Ben cheered, like we did when we had a big victory at the Medieval Renaissance Fair.

I helped Sophie up off the ground, wiped her tears away, and hugged her. It became a giant group hug.

Sophie whispered to me, "You don't have to be Paul Bunyan chopping down trees. You can use your brain and be resourceful. And there's nobody out here with as big a brain as you."

"Thanks," I said. "I do have a pretty big brain."

Sophie chuckled. "And apparently a big head, too," she said, referring to my ego.

But then the celebration ended abruptly when Sammie said, "Mr. Muscalini is unconscious again."

23

I stared at Mr. Muscalini in panic. I still had no idea how we were going to move him.

Nick said, "I don't think we can carry him."

"We can, but it has to be a team effort," I said.

I thought for a minute. I nodded to Nick and Jayden. "I need two pieces of wood, at least ten feet long. It's gotta be solid, but not too thick that we can't wrap our hands around it."

Just Charles asked, "What are you thinking?"

I didn't have time for questions. "Get me two sleeping bags."

Sammie tossed me hers. Luke followed with his.

"Nice. Unicorns and Star Wars." I nodded to Cheryl and Just Charles. "Zip them together. We're gonna make a stretcher with the wood."

Ditzy Dayna asked, "Where's Randy?"

"Let's just leave him," Cheryl said.

"We can't leave him," I said. I looked at Regan. She was on the verge of tears.

Derek said, "Are we sure about that?" He was probably

thinking about all the additional glory that would come his way without Randy on the ballfields with him.

"We can't go searching for him. We're running out of time. Mr. Muscalini is sick."

"We have to choose one or the other. And Randy made his choice," Jayden said.

Nick said, "Let's send out a signal."

"We don't have a signal," I said.

Luke said, "I wish we had the Bat signal."

"Well, if we can find a cave with bat guano in it and some potassium nitrate crystals, I can make a flare," I said, thinking.

"What is bat guano?" Ditzy Dayna asked.

Ben sang like an opera singer, "Guano. Guano. Guaaaannnnooooo!"

"Bat poop," I said.

"You want to make a poop flare, Davenfart? You can't make this stuff up," Randy said, reappearing.

"Welcome back, War*bear*macher," I said.

"Laugh if you want. I don't care. I just want to go home." Randy was defeated.

Randy walked over to Regan and whispered something to her. She turned her back on him. He took a deep breath and walked away.

I wasn't going to add to his misery. "Guys, we can fight all we want Nerds vs. Idiots when we get back," I said, before Nick interrupted me.

"Hey, who are the idiots?" Nick asked.

I continued without answering, "But this is bigger than middle school. We've got mayhem to deal with here and we need to work together if we're gonna make it out of this alive."

Ben laughed.

"What's so funny?" Sammie asked.

"We're all gonna die!" Ben yelled while smiling, which was really creepy.

Everyone's face dropped.

"Ignore him," I said. "He's been poisoned like Mr. Muscalini."

"I'm gonna die!" Ben yelled, thrusting his fists into the air.

Just Charles took out the soggy, smudged map. "I can barely make out some of this, but we have to move fast for the next four miles. We need to find the rest of the group and get Mr. Muscalini to safety."

Sammie knelt down and felt his head. "He feels warm." She felt Ben's head. "Him, too."

Ben sang once again, "The end is near for me!"

I said, "We've got to stay together. Charles, you've got so much gear, you're slowing us down and separating us. Let's leave everything behind that we don't need," I said.

Derek nodded to Randy. I chuckled.

"Canteens and survival gear only," I said.

"My mom is gonna be so mad if I leave her pots and pans."

"The bears can use them," Luke said.

"Bears can cook?" Dayna asked. "Wow. Evolution is crazy."

Just Charles looked like he was going to cry. "What about The Hulk?"

"You can keep The Hulk," I said.

"Got it, captain," Just Charles said, with a salute.

"And we've got to put our slowest people up front. Charles, Sophie, and Mr. Muscalini need to be at the head of the line. We go at their pace. That way we all stay together."

Luke said, unhelpfully, "I don't want to walk behind Ben. He's farting up a storm."

WE HAD two long pieces of wood running through the two sleeping bags, acting as a stretcher. Nick and Derek lined it up next to Mr. Muscalini. The two of them and Jayden rolled Mr. Muscalini onto the stretcher. He lay face down on it.

"We can't leave him face down," Sophie said. "He'll suffocate."

"Yeah, but I don't want him farting all over my sleeping bag. He'll burn a hole right through!" Luke said.

I shot Luke a look.

"Oh, all right," he said.

They flipped him over with a few grunts and groans.

"Let's move out," I said, waving everyone forward.

Mr. Muscalini coughed. We all stopped to see what was going to happen.

"He's trying to say something," Regan said, putting her ear to Mr. Muscalini's mouth.

Something definitely came out of his mouth, but it wasn't words per se, unless you count the "Hwuuulllaahhh!" Water gushed from Mr. Muscalini's mouth like a geyser, hitting Regan in the face with the force of a fire hose on full blast.

It reminded me of the first time we met Regan at Camp Cherriwacka. A kid named Sly opened a can of soda in her face after shaking it up. It was revenge for pushing Ben into the pool. But this was way cooler with puke. At least for us. The only thing better would've been a skunk. Regan fell back onto her butt, soaking wet. And demoralized.

Randy helped her up. She stood up and hugged him. He

looked half relieved that they had reconciled and half disgusted that she was all puked up. We hit the trail after a few minutes.

Thankfully, Ben didn't eat nearly as many berries as Mr. Muscalini did, but what he did consume was still having a delirious effect on him. Ben looked up at the trees above us, mesmerized. "Leaves. Le-ahhves. L' Aves."

"What is he talking about?" Sammie asked, concerned.

Sophie shrugged. "I think he's speaking French."

Ben said, "Fuuuhhhhrenchah."

Sammie said, "Ben, come back to us."

Ben looked at Sammie and smiled. "If you fart- faaahhh-harrrt- in the forrrrresssst and nobody else is arrrrround, does it still make a sssssound?"

"Ummm, not sure," Sammie said, seemingly disgusted, and speeding up.

Ben ripped a fart. It echoed through the woods.

"Gross," Sophie said, speeding up ahead.

"Imagine how I feel. I'm downwind!" Luke said.

"You deserve it," I said.

Ben caught back up to Sammie. He looked at her, dazed. "I just wove you, baby girl. Give your Benny Bear a smoochie smoochie."

Sammie rolled her eyes.

Luke passed by Sammie and Ben, catching up to Sophie and me. He leaned over and said, "I should've grabbed some of those berries. They seem to make everyone want to kiss. You mind if I double back? It could work wonders for me and Dayna."

I looked at him and said, "Dude."

"Okay. Okay."

WE HAD BEEN HIKING for about an hour. We stopped for a few minute break. Nick, Derek, and Jayden looked like their hands were about to fall off from gripping the stretcher for so long. Even though we were tired, since we hadn't been attacked by the Boogie Man, Big Foot, or any more bears, so I was pretty pleased.

Until Just Charles said, "Mr. Muscalini doesn't look good."

"I don't want to get too close," Sophie said. She leaned her head back while trying to feel Mr. Muscalini's forehead with her hand. "He's burning up. We've got to hurry."

Mr. Muscalini let a fart rip.

"I want my sleeping bag back," Luke said.

"You can wash it," Cheryl said.

Luke shook his head, "He farted on Luke Skywalker. That's unforgivable."

"Let's worry about it after we get home," I said.

"Easy to say when it's not your sleeping bag he's farting on," Luke said, angrily.

Derek walked over to me and said, "I'm not sure how much longer we can carry him. He's pretty heavy. My hands and forearms are shot."

"Mine, too," Nick said.

I took a deep breath. "Okay," I said, thinking. "Do we have any belts?"

The group answered a collective, "No."

"What do we have?" I asked.

Just Charles said, "Rope, bungee cords, backpacks, and some clothes."

"Hmmm," I said. "What if we used the clothes as padding and you walked with the stretcher on your shoulders?"

Derek said, "Nick is a bit taller than we are, but not enough that we can't make it work."

"Nick is the only one who can hold a side by himself," Jayden said. "But if the three of us rotate, two at a time, I think we can do it," he said, referring to himself, Derek, and Randy. None of the nerds could carry Mr. Muscalini. As soon as the stretcher let down on one of our shoulders, we'd be driven into the ground like a tent stake.

Sophie said, "We've gotta hurry."

I looked at the map. "We just have to make it to the pass and then we should be home free."

The boys hoisted Mr. Muscalini's stretcher onto the shoulders of Nick, Jayden, and Randy. They led the way down the path. We hiked for another two hours, stopping here and there, with the football players taking turns carrying the stretcher.

Nick called out, "How much longer?" He sounded like he was going to need his own stretcher in a minute or two.

"According to this map, it should be right down this path," I said, pointing to a path that was not as worn as the trail we had been on, but was clearly used.

I hustled ahead of the group to make sure we were going in the right direction. The sound of the river grew louder as we approached.

Sophie sidled up next to me. "Ummm, I thought you said there was a foot bridge. They look more like stepping stones and half of them are missing."

"That's what Ron told me," I said. "They're not missing. The river is just too high. They're submerged."

"What's the problem?" Randy asked.

"It's flooded," I said.

There was no way we were going to be able to cross the river with Mr. Muscalini. We were doomed yet again.

24

W e stood at the edge of the river, looking across to the other side. It was so close, yet so far.

Sammie said, "We just gotta power through it. We're almost there."

I said, "We have to think about this first."

"All we have to do is get to the other side," Sophie said, to herself. "Easier said than done."

Randy stepped forward. "All *I* have to do is get to the other side...I don't need you to do that." He looked at Regan. "Let's go," he said, simply.

"Really, *Captain?*" Derek questioned.

Randy ignored him and stepped out onto the first rock, which was about six inches submerged. He looked into the water and hopped to the next one, barely keeping his balance. Regan followed behind him.

"This could work," Jayden said.

"If we leave Mr. Muscalini behind," Derek said.

I shook my head. I couldn't believe they were thinking of leaving Mr. Muscalini behind.

Derek continued, "Which we're not doing."

I exhaled. I was proud that my brother wasn't going the selfish route. He was pretty good at it. Actually, he was an expert.

Before we could come up with a plan, Randy shrieked. He wobbled on the rocks, appeared to regain his footing, and then slipped and fell into the rapids. He reached out a hand, which Regan grabbed. Randy's force pulled her into the water. The two of them clung to a rock as the river water blasted them, threatening to wash them down the river without life jackets.

"Help me!" Randy yelled.

I looked at Just Charles. "Get the rope out!"

Randy and Regan started to inch their fingers along the rocks, back toward us.

Just Charles took out the rope, handed it to Nick, and said, "Make sure you hold onto the end. It's a frequent beginner's mistake."

Nick nodded, wrapped the end of the rope around his hand, and tossed the rest of the coil too Randy and Regan. They each grabbed on with one hand and then with the other. The water swung them away from the submerged bridge. Nick reeled them in, hand over fist, until the two moronic middle schoolers climbed up the river bank and back onto dry land. Although deservedly, they were soaking wet.

Randy said a sheepish, "Thanks."

Derek muttered, "Idiots." I couldn't have agreed more.

Just Charles said, "Maybe we can start a fire and signal the crew. We're close enough that they could see smoke."

I looked up into the air. "It's too cloudy. They won't notice it. Plus, they might not even know it was ours."

Luke said, "Too bad you don't have a flare gun in there, Charles."

Sammie asked, "Are you sure you don't?"

Just Charles said, "Yeah, pretty sure."

Derek asked curiously, "Why did you need your Hulk action figure, Zaino?"

"That's none of your business. I advise you to stay out of my personal affairs," Just Charles snapped.

Derek rolled his eyes at Jayden and muttered, "Nerds."

"Man, if we only had some bat poop," I said, pounding my fist into my hand.

Sophie looked at me and said, "You've said some really weird things over the years, but that might be the weirdest."

I shrugged. "Bat poop would be very helpful here. I will defend that to my dying day."

"Ha, ha! That's today!" Ben yelled.

"What do we have to work with?" Nick asked.

"Look around the grounds here. It can be anything. Like a rock. Nothing is too obvious," I said.

Everybody spread out, searching for something to help us get across the river.

Sammie said, "There's an old campsite over here. There's a fire pit. A few arrows in that tree."

Ben gave a thumbs up and said, "See! I told you we're all gonna die!" He grabbed a fist full of grass and ran it through his fingers. "Well, you guys are, anyway." He stared at the grass. "Grrrrrraaaaasss."

"Too bad we can't build that human catapult we designed for the science fair," I said to Ben.

"Cat-a-pullllt. That's funny," Ben said, unhelpfully.

"What else do we have?" Sophie asked.

Just Charles shook his head. "A whole lot of nothing."

"Not true," I said, tapping my chin. I looked at Derek, Nick, and Jayden. "Can you guys try to get those arrows out of the tree without breaking the arrowheads?"

They nodded and headed over to the tree.

"Charles, I need a stick, about three feet, and not too thick. It has to flex a little bit when bent."

Just Charles nodded. "Got it."

I looked at Sophie. "And you, my lady, are key to this plan."

"What do you want me to do?" she asked.

"I need you to harness Medieval Sophie," I said, referring to our time at the Renaissance Fair when she crushed the archery contest and took out Randy and Regan with suction-cupped arrows to the forehead. It was spectacular. But this was real life.

"Okay," she said, uncertain.

"Don't worry," I said, reaching into Just Charles' pack and pulling out a bungee cord.

Sophie frowned. "What's that for?"

Just Charles returned with a perfect-looking stick. "You can never have too many bungee cords. They're the better cousin of duct tape."

"That's what you say. Let's not get carried away here, but it should do the trick," I said. "Now, I need the axe."

"You sure about this?" Sophie asked, uneasily.

I nodded. "I am, but if it makes everyone feel more comfortable, I'll have Derek do it."

Everyone within earshot screamed, "Yes!"

Derek, Nick, and Jayden returned with two arrows, fully intact.

"Noyce!" I said. "Great work."

I handed Derek the stick. "Can you use the axe to notch out a little rut in the top and bottom?"

"Yep."

Derek took the axe and carefully carved out the two notches. He held the stick up for me. I took a bungee cord and used the hooks to secure it to the stick, turning it into a bow.

"I see where you're going with this," Sophie said, taking a deep breath.

"Can you slice the rope in two and secure each piece to the arrows?" I asked Derek.

Derek took the axe and chopped the rope in half. Jayden and Sammie each took a piece and tied it around the arrows, just in front of the feathers.

I looked around. "We need two more sticks, dug into the ground here and here," I said, pointing to the river bank just in front of the first step of the foot bridge. "They should be four feet tall or so. We'll tie the other end of the rope to these."

Luke and Just Charles returned with the sticks. Derek grabbed them and used the butt of the axe to hammer the sticks firmly into the ground. Cheryl and Sammie tied knots around the two sticks.

I handed the bow and an arrow to Sophie and said, "Do your thing."

Sophie nodded and took a deep breath. She buried the arrow head in the mud and tested the bungee cord. Nobody said a word. Even Randy kept his mouth shut, which was a surprise. Sophie pulled the arrow from the ground, wiped the tip clean, and then nocked the arrow. She raised the bow and steadied the arrow, as she pulled back the bungee cord. It was a little unsteady and a bit windy.

I stood directly behind Sophie. She aimed for the closest tree, directly across from us. She let go of the arrow. It was so effortless, it was almost anticlimactic. The feathers on the arrow brushed against her cheek, as the arrow surged toward its target, arced over the river, and sunk into the intended target with a thwack. We all cheered, not realizing that the taut rope uprooted the stick anchoring the rope to our side.

"No!" I yelled, diving for the stick.

I was on my stomach, the stick loosely in my fingers. That's when the mayhem broke out. Apparently, when football players see people around them diving for stuff, they join in for fun.

Derek yelled, "Fumble!" He promptly dove on top of me, his chest smashing me in the back of the head.

Before I knew what had happened, Nick, Randy, and Jayden all joined the fray.

I was pummeled with knees, elbows, and fists. Somebody even gave me a purple nurple. I'm sure it was Randy. The weight crushed my bones and half buried me in the mud.

With a mouthful of mud, I yelled, "Ra floof kiffing me?"

I think they all thought I said something about kissing me, so they rolled off quickly. I inhaled, but held my breath. I slowly opened one eye, knowing that I no longer held the stick. I hoped someone else had grabbed it from me.

Derek held the stick above his head like he had just made the game-saving fumble recovery.

"I had it," I said, wiping the mud from my face.

"Sorry, it's an automatic reflex," Derek said.

"Okay. Let's try it again. This time, can someone secure the stick before she lets the arrow fly?" I said.

Jayden said, "I got it." He sat down behind the stick and held it with both hands.

I handed Sophie the second arrow. She grabbed it from me, nocked it, and readied her bow. I took a step back, as she aimed for a tree three feet to the right of the first arrow. Sophie let the arrow fly. A gust of wind pushed the arrow left. We all arced our bodies toward the target, willing the arrow into the tree. I leaned so far, I almost fell over. We contorted ourselves like a bunch of wannabe yoga masters. The arrow cut through the soggy tree bark and buried its tip with a beautiful thwack.

We all cheered and then engulfed Sophie in a hug. Well, except for Randy and Regan.

I elbowed Nick in the ribs. Gently. "That's my girl."

I thought he might kill me, but he nodded and said, "That's one bad chick."

"Who's going first?" Cheryl asked, uneasily.

I looked across the river. Even with two ropes stretching across the river as a wobbly handrail, it was a daunting task. The strength of the water had been enough to knock Randy and Regan off the bridge.

"We should go one at a time, except somebody should

go with Ben and two people are gonna have to carry Mr. Muscalini across."

"That looks shaky," Regan said. "I don't know if that's gonna hold."

Derek stepped forward. "I'll go first. My brother is the smartest kid I know. It'll hold."

I looked away, not wanting to anyone to see me tearing up. It wasn't often my brother supported me. And I was at my emotional wits end.

"What's his GPA?" Randy asked, defensively.

Everyone yelled in unison, "Shut up, Randy!"

I stepped in front of Derek. "I made it. I'll go first. And I'll be reminding you for the rest of your life what you just said."

"I already regret it," Derek said, with a playful smirk.

I went first, carefully navigating the submerged bridge. The white rapids pummeled my legs, but with the rope handrails, I was able to keep my balance. I had never felt so good about stepping into a pile of mud as when I stepped out of the water on the other side of the river. I turned around to watch the rest of the crew follow. One by one, and a three by one, our group passed over the angry, rotten river to safety. Or at least to a substance that was non toxic.

WE WERE in the home stretch. We hit the hiking trails for the final few minutes. All we had to do was cut across to the shore of the fork we missed during the rafting trip. We were battered and bruised. We were starving and soaking wet. We had been poisoned, bitten by venomous snakes, nearly struck by lightning and killed by a falling tree, eaten by a bear, drowned in a mud slide, and nearly lost appendages due to VERY slippery axe handles. Yet, we had a bounce in our step, as we approached our final destination.

And then, through the trees, we saw it. A sign read, 'Rocky River Rafting Adventures'.

"We're here!" I yelled.

We walked down the path to a small hut. There were no signs of activity anywhere. No rafts. No people. No buses. Nothing.

"Where is everybody?" Sophie asked.

"They were supposed to be here," I said, looking at the map.

Sammie asked, "Did something happen to them?"

Ben looked around, smiled, and then yelled, "We're all gonna die!" It echoed through the trees.

And it was those words that saved us all.

I heard something in the brush. I looked toward the sound, the sun blaring into my eyes. I looked down to avoid the sunlight and saw a hulking shadow. Sophie saw it as well.

She said, "Another bear..."

My knees shook. I had already scared away one bear, but how lucky could a kid like me be in bear encounters? We had made it all that way and it was all going to end in a feast, and we were the meal.

25

A s the figure got closer, I realized it was not a bear, but Colt Reddington! I had never loved and hated someone so much at the same time.

Colt rushed over to us and said, "Thank goodness! We found you!"

"You found us?" I asked.

After all we had been through, I took it as a personal affront, but I let it go as we were finally where we needed to be and safe.

"We thought the worst," Colt said. "The rest of the group is at the main launch, just through the brush. We heard your scream!"

Ms. Armpit Hair burst through the brush and rushed to us. She threw her arms around me and squeezed as tight as she could. I hugged her back. We were so excited to be alive, and she was probably excited that she wasn't going to definitely lose her job, that we both had forgotten how much we hated each other. It did make for an awkward parting once we remembered.

She looked at me, her eyes knowing that we should not

have done that given our history, and moved me to the side by my shoulders. She then proceeded to shake hands with the rest of the crew, which was kind of strange, but better than hugging her, I guess.

And then Mr. Muscalini sat up. "What the-? Why does my face hurt? Where are we? Unicorns? I don't have a unicorn sleeping bag!"

We all rushed to Mr. Muscalini and tackled him. It was a giant football pileup, without the football, but all of the disgusting smells, and probably a few more. Even Randy joined in. And I'm pretty certain he stunk just as bad as the rest of us, although I'm sure he would deny it.

We eventually got up and helped Mr. Muscalini to his feet. He wobbled a bit, but leaned on Nick for support.

Cheryl said, "You were bitten by a snake. How are you okay?"

Mr. Muscalini said, "My metabolism burns hotter than a volcano. I must've burned that snake poison for fuel."

"That's one bad dude," Colt said.

Ms. Armpit Hair said, "You should get checked out in the hospital anyway. For liability, err just to be safe."

"Nonsense," Mr. Muscalini said.

"Please, Mr. Muscalini," we all said.

Mr. Muscalini huffed. "Oh, all right." He looked down to his side, seemingly about to say something deep. Tears welled up in his eyes. "I...missed you. I thought I might never see you again."

Sophie said, "Aww, Mr. Muscalini. We missed you, too."

Mr. Muscalini looked up and frowned. "What? Oh, I wasn't talking to you. I was talking to my bulging biceps. Still look good even after a starvation diet."

We all shook our heads and chuckled, as Mr. Muscalini flexed, admiring his two best friends.

Colt said, "Well, let's hurry over. The rest of the group will be dying to see you." I thought it was a poor choice of words, but I wasn't going to argue with him.

We emerged from the brush, like a scene out of a movie. A bad one. We walked together in slow motion, not because the director wanted special effects, but because we were so broken and tired, that was all the strength we could muster. Sophie hobbled on her twisted ankle. Ben was still delirious, barely able to stand up. Derek, Nick, and Jayden were so exhausted, they leaned on each other as they walked.

Half the eighth-grade class surged forward, engulfing us in hugs and pummeling us with questions. It felt like I hadn't seen them in years.

After the mayhem died down, I looked up at Colt. "Any word from Mr. Gifford and Mrs. Funderbunk? Are they with you?"

Colt lowered his head. "No. I don't...think they...made it."

"What?" Sophie asked, fighting back tears.

The celebration ended abruptly. I couldn't believe it. We had been through so much and thought we had made it back safely, only to find out that our two teachers hadn't survived.

Sophie buried her head in my chest. I cried into her frizzy curls.

"I can't...believe this," I said, barely able to control myself.

And then we heard a rustle in the trees.

"Is that a bear?" Randy asked, his knees knocking.

Dayna shrieked, "I think it's a shark!"

Colt pushed us back, protecting us. "Stand back, kids. I'll take care of this."

Somebody farted. It was bad timing, but it's natural.

"Maybe it's a barking tree frog," I suggested.

It was none of those things, particularly not a shark. Emerging from the brush, dirty from head to toe, but a new man, was one Mr. Gifford. He carried Mrs. Funderbunk in his arms with hers wrapped around his neck. Mr. Gifford let Mrs. Funderbunk down gently onto the ground.

We all rushed and engulfed them in a giant hug.

Mr. Gifford reached for me and pulled me in tight. "Austin, my boy! It's so good to see you!"

They were some of the smelliest hugs I'd ever been involved in, but also some of the best. I could barely speak, I was so relieved, as we celebrated.

ONCE WE ALL calmed down and told our crazy survival stories, Ms. Armpit Hair stepped forward, forcing a smile onto her face. "Well, wasn't that exciting?" she said, as if it was some sort of joyous event and not the class trip of doom. "I think we had too much fun. Don't you?"

"This is going to be a Broadway hit!" Mrs. Funderbunk sang, beaming.

Nobody else answered.

"Don't you?" she asked, angrily.

A few people nodded.

"We'll be boarding the bus in just a few minutes. I think we had so much fun, we shouldn't tell our parents about any of this. I'd hate for you to be the cause of the whole school getting detention for a month."

I looked over at Mr. Gifford. He was beaming, while holding hands with Mrs. Funderbunk. I walked over to him and whispered, "What happened out there?"

He leaned down and whispered back, "A wise man once said, 'There's something primal about camping.' I became a man out there, Austin."

I was really confused. I was certain he was the person he was quoting, but he called himself a wise man, then said he became a man, but at the time he said it, he would've been a boy or even a baby.

"Austin, you okay?"

I smiled. "Yep. Never better. I just want to get home to see my family. And eat!"

Mr. Muscalini said, "Hey, look! There are berries over there!"

Our whole group yelled in unison, "Nooooooo!"

26

B en and Mr. Muscalini got a separate ride straight to
the hospital for tests and treatment, but they were
expected to be okay. I fell asleep on Sophie's
shoulder on the bus ride home. We were all exhausted.
Physically, mentally, spiritually, emotionally, nutritionally,
and aquatically. Sophie shook me awake, as the bus pulled
into the parking lot. I looked around, still half asleep. I
noticed a gob of spit that I had left in Sophie's hair, but I
decided to leave it. She had so much junk in her curls that I
was convinced my spit actually made it look better. I was
also half afraid to stick my hand in there for fear that I
would be attacked by a rabid squirrel or something.

Our parents waited for us on the sidewalk in front of the
school. As we approached, the crowd broke out into cheers.
My sleepiness disappeared as energy surged through my
body, longing to see my parents. And possibly eat my mother's pocketbook. How much worse could leather taste
compared to the cafeteria food?

Our bus screeched to a stop. We all bounced up and into
the aisles, jockeying to be the first off the bus and as far

away from the disastrous trip as possible. But before we could exit, Ms. Armpit Hair walked up the steps of the bus.

Ms. Armpit Hair looked at the bus driver and said, "Shut the door."

The driver did as he was told.

Ms. Armpit Hair looked at us and said, "Remember now, students. Don't tell anyone about this, particularly your parents. Unless you want detention for the rest of the year. What happened at Rocky River stays at Rocky River. Or else."

We all nodded in agreement and surged off the bus behind her. And of course, the first thing we all did was describe to our parents just how horrible the whole thing was.

"Mommy! We almost got eaten by a bear!" Randy yelled. He sobbed, as he buried his head on his mother's shoulder.

"A tree almost killed us!" I yelled to my parents.

Derek celebrated, "Austin didn't get eaten by a bear! Randy owes me ten bucks!" He looked at Randy and said, "Boom, sucka!"

Regan told her parents, "I almost drowned!"

Michael Norton apparently had faulty information. "Mr. Muscalini's dead!"

Parents stormed up to Ms. Armpit Hair. There was so much yelling, all of the words meshed into one cacophonous complaint. Ms. Armpit Hair tried to calm them down, but the negative energy seemed to fuel her blood pressure higher and higher. I was half concerned that she might Kung-Fu chop some parent and half hoping she would. Even though I was leaving Cherry Avenue Middle School in a matter of months, I wished she would get fired. She had no business supervising children. And that was my belief even before the Rotten River trip.

My mother inspected me, I guess making sure all of me had returned home.

"Are you okay, my baby?" my mother asked, and then did the same to Derek.

I nodded. "Mom, I'm fine. I'm not a baby."

She stared at me, as if assessing something new. "You have a look in your eye."

I shrugged. "It's just my eyes."

"No, you look more confident," she said.

My father raised an eyebrow. "Older, even."

"I guess I grew up a little on the trip. I mean, I'm not ready to quit school and work in the mines or anything, but I do feel a bit more mature."

"He saved us all," Derek said.

I looked at my parents. "I think we have a problem." I leaned in and whispered, "This boy is impersonating my brother."

We all laughed.

My mom grabbed me by the shoulders and said, "I'm sorry I said I couldn't wait for you to leave. Without you, there would be a hole in my heart. You want to know where you fit in in this family? Just be you. Nobody has your smarts and your sense of humor."

"That is true," I said.

"Let's get out of here," my father said. "This crowd is getting hostile."

I looked over to see Ms. Armpit Hair, still fielding questions and insults.

As we walked away from the crowd, I heard Randy say, "And a tree almost fell on me, but I risked my life to save Austin."

Mrs. Warblemacher shrieked, "My boy is a hero?"

I just shook my head and chuckled.

We stopped to check in with the rest of my crew.

I leaned in toward Sophie and whispered, "Let's never do that again."

She laughed and then feigned surprise. "What? Why would you say that? You're the Paul Bunyan of nerds."

I scoffed. "Nerd? What are you talking about? How about environmental genius?"

"More like the teenage axe murderer," Sophie said, with a chuckle.

"I don't even want to know," my mother said.

Just Charles' mom tried to wipe his face. "Ma, I got it. But thank you."

I gave Sophie a hug. Out of the corner of my eye, I spotted Mr. Gifford and Mrs. Funderbunk kissing.

My eyes widened.

They parted and Mr. Gifford said, "I'm not so sure we should kiss in front of the children."

Mrs. Funderbunk looked up at him and said, "When you have what we have, it's not something you can hide! Pucker up, stud muffin." She pulled him in by his shirt and laid one on him. A big one.

It was kinda gross, to be honest. I mean, hadn't we all gotten wet enough? The slobber was off the charts. But I was happy for Mr. Gifford. After the wet and lengthy kiss, he looked at me, smiling ear to ear. His eyes bulged as Mrs. Funderbunk grabbed him by the shirt again and tugged him forward into her lips.

I looked over at Sophie and whispered, "That'll be us, someday. Singing show tunes and sloppy smoochie smoochie."

"Oh, God. No," she said, laughing.

I shrugged. "I don't like show tunes all that much, either."

27

After we got settled at home and ate so much I almost puked, my family went to visit Ben and Mr. Muscalini in the hospital. When we arrived in the visitor area, Ben was on his way out. He walked over to us with his parents.

"You okay?" I asked.

Ben shook his head. "Totally. Toaaaahhhhtaaaallly," he said.

My eyes widened. Ben burst out laughing.

"Gotcha!"

I rolled my eyes. "Good one, dude."

Mrs. Gordon said, "Let's get you something to eat."

"Yes," he said. "Anything I want, right?"

"Anything for my baby," Mrs. Gordon said.

Ben looked at me and said, "I'm not a baby. But we goin' Frankie's. We goin' Frankie's," referring to our favorite pizza place.

We said our goodbyes and headed to see Mr. Muscalini. I led us into room 44, which was fitting, given that Mr. Muscalini's favorite football play was the 44 Blast.

The hulking phys ed teacher laughed as he watched some sort of reality TV show. His eyes bulged when he saw us. He scrambled to find the remote and shut the TV off.

"I must've dozed off. Not sure what this even is," he said, his cheeks reddening.

Leighton said, "Can you believe Jessica is still into Donovan after all he did?"

Mr. Muscalini said, "I know, right. What a jerk! I mean-"

"How are you?" I asked, sidling up to his hospital bed. He looked odd in the paisley gown.

"They say I'll be fine soon," Mr. Muscalini said. He looked at Derek and said, "Tell anybody about my hospital gown and you won't be the captain of the baseball team anymore."

Derek looked confused. "Sir, I'm not the captain of the baseball team."

"You are now. Randy's not ready."

Derek was beaming. "I won't let you down."

Usually, I hated it when my brother got accolades, but I was okay with this one. Maybe because he called me a genius.

I looked at Mr. Muscalini's face. There was a Band Aid covering the snake bite, but there was still some swelling. "The swelling is getting better," I said.

Mr. Muscalini smiled. "I finally got that butt chin I always wanted."

"Enjoy it while it lasts," I said.

Mr. Muscalini's lip quivered. Thankfully, he avoided tears. I empathized with him. At least he got to experience what it was like to have a butt chin. True, he was poisoned and got bitten by a venomous snake, but still.

Mr. Muscalini looked at my parents said, "I'm proud of your son. He manned up and took charge. He was a leader."

"We're very proud of Derek," my mother said.

Mr. Muscalini shook his head. "I was talking about Austin. If he didn't stink so much at sports, he would be a captain on one of my teams, for sure."

"Thank you?" my father said, not sure how much of a compliment it actually was.

Mr. Muscalini looked at me. "You took care of all of us. We wouldn't have made it back without you."

I nodded. "I just did what I thought was right."

My dad pat me on the shoulder. "We're proud of you, son. Even though you stink at sports."

I laughed. "I'm actually thinking of learning a new sport," I said.

Mr. Muscalini's eyes lit up. "What's that?"

"Axe throwing," I said, trying not to laugh.

"You're so lucky Sophie's not here," Derek said, laughing.

"I don't want to know," my mother said.

Mr. Muscalini said, "Thanks for coming."

He shook my hand, nearly crushing it. I was grateful we were already in the hospital, because I was pretty certain I needed an x-ray. I was also grateful that Mr. Muscalini didn't get up to see us out. I had no interest in seeing him stand up in his gown. I had seen enough horror that weekend to last me until my dying day. I didn't need to see his butt, too. It might have actually killed me.

On the way out of the hospital, I said, "I'm hungry."

My father suggested, "Burger Boys?"

"Why don't we just grill some burgers ourselves?" Derek said. "Austin and I can fire up the grill."

I looked at him and smirked.

"What? Too soon?" he asked.

"Nah, I think we can make mom and dad dinner and save them a few bucks. I'm sure you'll crash the car one day and cost them a ton of money," I said, patting Derek on the shoulder.

"Will not," Derek argued. "Well, maybe. But you're the one who destroyed a bridge."

My parents looked at us, not sure what to say. "What kind of class trip did you go on?"

"It was more of a life quest," I said.

Derek said, "It was almost a life*less* quest."

"I don't think we should talk about this anymore," my mother said.

"Yeah, I think I need therapy," I said.

Derek rolled his eyes, jokingly. "You needed it long before this trip."

I looked at my parents. "You should probably take us to Crescent Cove, so we can decompress."

My dad smiled. "Sure. You guys can pay with your new jobs."

"What?" we both shrieked.

"We have a baby coming. We're not going on vacation, but since you're all grown up now, it's time you two get a job."

Aaaaahhh, farts.

Got Audio?

Want to listen to Middle School Mayhem?

ABOUT THE AUTHOR

C.T. Walsh is the author of the Middle School Mayhem Series, set to be a total twelve hilarious adventures of Austin Davenport and his friends.

Besides writing fun, snarky humor and the occasionally-frequent fart joke, C.T. loves spending time with his family, coaching his kids' various sports, and successfully turning seemingly unsandwichable things into spectacular sandwiches, while also claiming that he never eats carbs. He assures you, it's not easy to do. C.T. knows what you're thinking: this guy sounds complex, a little bit mysterious, and maybe even dashingly handsome, if you haven't been to the optometrist in a while. And you might be right.

C.T. finds it weird to write about himself in the third person, so he is going to stop doing that now.

You can learn more about C.T. (oops) at ctwalsh.fun

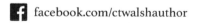 facebook.com/ctwalshauthor

ALSO BY C.T. WALSH

Middle School Mayhem Series

Down with the Dance: Book One

Santukkah!: Book Two

The Science (Un)Fair: Book Three

Battle of the Bands: Book Four

Medieval Mayhem: Book Five

The Takedown: Book Six

Valentine's Duh: Book Seven

The Comic Con: Book Eight

Election Misdirection: Book Nine

Education Domestication: Book Ten

Future Release schedule

Graduation Detonation: November 15th, 2020

Picture Books

The 250-Year-Old Bride

The Kung Pao Cow

Who Hides Under Monsters' Beds?

47163637R00115